**A DIMPY GRUAR MYSTERY**

# A MANOR OF MURDER

**WENDY LAING**

This is an IndieMosh book

brought to you by MoshPit Publishing
an imprint of Mosher's Business Support Pty Ltd

PO Box 147
Hazelbrook NSW 2779

indiemosh.com.au

Copyright © Wendy Laing 2020

The moral right of the author has been asserted in accordance with the Copyright Amendment (Moral Rights) Act 2000.

All rights reserved. Except as permitted under the Australian Copyright Act 1968 (for example, fair dealing for the purposes of study, research, criticism or review) no part of this publication may be reproduced, stored in a retrieval system, or transmitted in any form or by any means, electronic, mechanical, photocopying, recording or otherwise, without the written permission of the publisher.

A catalogue record for this work is available from the National Library of Australia

https://www.nla.gov.au/collections

| Title: | A Manor of Murder |
|---|---|
| Author: | Laing, Wendy |
| ISBNs: | 978-1-922440-84-6 (paperback) |
| Subjects: | FICTION: General; Mystery & Detective / Women Sleuths: Mystery & Detective / Amateur Sleuth; Crime |

This story is entirely a work of fiction. No character in this story is taken from real life. Any resemblance to any person or persons living or dead is accidental and unintentional. The author, their agents and publishers cannot be held responsible for any claim otherwise and take no responsibility for any such coincidence.

Cover concept by Wendy Laing
Cover design and layout by Ally Mosher at allymosher.com
Cover images from Adobe Stock

# Acknowledgements

A big thank you to my two readers, Ros Sydes and Erin Eiffe, and Sally Odgers, my editor and assessor for their support and encouragement.

# Chapter 1

Eleven-thirty on a wintry Tuesday night. Propped up in bed with a mystery novel; my reading came to an abrupt stop when I heard the muffled thump. I had read the last few lines a dozen times without taking in any of the story. My eyes felt gritty, despite best efforts to focus on the words.

The dull thud meant Carol Wilson, who has the apartment next to mine at the Mountain View Residential Manor, had fallen out of bed again.

I listened for a few minutes, and all seemed quiet, but it had shattered my concentration. To continue reading was impossible and there would be no sleep until I helped Carol back into bed.

Carol is one of my friends at the Manor and has been since we arrived on the same day three years ago. Nevertheless, friendship or not, this habit of falling out of bed had to stop.

The noise would also have woken other residents. Not that it made any difference. They'd snuggle under their blankets and expect me to crawl out of a warm bed and go to her aid. For some unknown reason, everyone presumed I'm an expert with anything out of the ordinary.

When I first made my home at the Manor, word passed around on the grapevine that I wrote romance novels. The books are fiction, the stories fantasy, but it made no difference. The *Carol falling out of bed* problem had become mine to solve.

I tossed the book onto the bedside table, sat on the edge of the bed and sighed. Someone needed to check she was okay. I was the designated someone.

My dressing gown hung on a hook beside the door. I took it down and shrugged it on over my nightie. Then scuffed my feet into slippers, opened the door and walked into the corridor.

All seemed quiet; as I hurried to Carol's apartment, knocked, opened the unlocked door and switched on the light. My eyes took in the twisted mass of bright pink sheets, and a purple hibiscus flowered doona which lay on the floor beside the bed.

Carol lay in the pile of bedclothes, tangled and dishevelled; nightdress crunched up to her chin. Dribble formed in the corner of her mouth which hung open as if in shock. Without bothering to shut the door, I skirted past the TV cabinet and lounge chairs and walked over to the bed.

In the past, she'd always had something to say, "Sorry, Dimpy," the name everyone calls me – or "Oops, I've done it again." Not this time. Instead, she stared into space with a weird, vacant expression. Perhaps she hit her head on the bedside table as she fell.

As I was about to shake her shoulders, a raspy, half-barking sound came from the corridor. It shattered the quietness and increased in volume as it approached Carol's apartment. Eyes wide and mouth agape in astonishment, I watched Barry Jackson lurch in the open doorway. Naked, except for a pair of baggy green silk shorts stencilled with cartoon characters, he clung onto the door handle to stop falling over.

Sweat covered his face, his body shook, and his back heaved as he coughed a series of hacking rasps which reached from deep in his chest.

Weird urk, urk sounds came from his mouth as it flew open

to release a stream of gas. A dead-earth smell wafted through Carol's bedroom. A queasy feeling rose in my throat and threatened to erupt at any moment. Stay where you are, I told the nausea, I've got enough problems.

Skinny arms clutched to his chest; his blue eyes stretched and frantic, Barry let go of the door handle and staggered forward into the room. His head swivelled towards me, but without saying a word, did a half pirouette, and fell face-down onto the floor next to Carol and lay still.

I ignored my stomach, knelt on the carpet alongside Barry and turned him over onto his back. "Barry," I said. "What's the matter? Can you hear me?" and to my shame, I noticed the upturned soles of his feet needed a good wash.

I lifted his wrist to find a pulse. What was the revival procedure? My memory remained a complete blank. Nothing about resuscitation came to mind. I placed my ear next to Barry's mouth and listened. Still no sound, but there was a thin stream of air on my cheek. Energised by the sign of life, I shook his shoulders.

His pale blue eyes opened and stared into my brown ones. He sighed, then made a half bullfrog croaking noise, "Urk!" His lips moved as he struggled to say something else, but all that came out were more choking urk sounds.

Now at my wit's end, I sat back on my heels and wondered what to do. My heart pounded while an unpleasant feeling crept into my stomach. Here I knelt on creaky knees, an oldish lady, mind in a considerable muddle bending over a man who sounded like a chicken. To make matters worse, Carol lay nearby in a tangle of sheets and doona, silent and still.

Barry was another resident of the Manor. Not a close friend, more of an acquaintance, – someone to say hello to at meal-times, or have a chat about trivial things when we met in the corridor. What had caused him to end up passed out on Carol's carpet? Had he also heard the thump, leaped out of bed and came to investigate? Could the sudden movement have caused a heart attack?

I put my ear against his mouth once more, but this time no sound occurred, not even an "urk". "Geez, Barry, you're not going to die, are you?" My body trembled with fear. What was I to do? My thought processes are not fast at the best of times and twelve-thirty in the night was not one of them.

Words flickered through my head: help, nurse, doctor, ambulance, phone.

I stood up and walked over to the bed, rummaged around under Carol's reading glasses and magazines on the bedside table and picked up her mobile phone. With shaky hands, I rang triple 0, told the operator someone had collapsed, and an ambulance needed to be sent to the Mountain View Residential Manor as quickly as possible.

My next call, I decided, should be to the manager of the Manor. About to check Carol's phone list for her number, a familiar voice came from the corridor.

"What on earth is going on, Dimpy?" There came a chuckle. "Are you having an orgy?"

# Chapter 2

I heaved a sigh of relief.

The person belonging to the voice stood in the doorway and gazed at the scene in front of her.

Dressed in night attire and slippers, Barbara Wakefield, our stocky, a tad overweight but efficient manager of the Mountain View Residential Manor had come to my rescue.

She walked into the room while continuing to speak. "I was lying awake in bed, reading the last chapter of my book, when noises filtered along the corridor. It's part of my job to check disturbances, so here I am." Hands on hips, she frowned at me. "Although, I was about to find out who the murderer was in my novel."

An expression of surprise appeared as she took a closer look at the two bodies lying on the floor.

"No, we're not having an orgy, Barbara," I answered as I replaced the phone onto the bedside table. "Carol fell out of bed again. I came here to untangle her from this mess of sheets and the doona. In the middle of doing that, Barry Jackson staggered in the door and collapsed onto the floor." A note of anxiety crept into my voice. "Barry made some funny noises and found it hard to take a breath while I was checking him. Is it possible he's had a heart attack? Could you examine him to make sure he is still breathing while I help Carol?"

My bottom lip trembled as I tried to remember what else I had done. "Oh, yes, I've rung the ambulance. It was out on a call, but the dispatcher assured me it would be here as soon as possible."

Barbara listened as I spoke and nodded a few times. "Calm down Dimpy; I've been trained to use cardiopulmonary resuscitation. Would you check Carol's okay while I tend to Barry," she said as she knelt on the carpet next to him.

"Yes, I can do that," I replied, relieved someone capable would deal with the situation.

I stood up, moved nearer to Carol and gazed down at her. A massive shape of what resembled a half-wrapped mummy lay on the carpet. Two big fat legs stuck out an edge of the jumble of sheets and the doona, her head and one arm out the other end. A picture came into my head of an albino beached whale.

A muffled voice came from the whale as her legs kicked and flailed at the sheets, "Is that you Dimpy? Did I bloody fall out of bed again?"

"Yes, it's me," I answered, shaking the whale image from my head. "and yes, you did bloody fall out of bed again. This has got to stop, Carol. You need to either buy a bigger bed or go on a diet. I can't keep doing this each time you roll over and land on the floor in the middle of the night."

Carol is seventy-five and obese, but she sees herself as somewhat on the plump side. The single bed she sleeps in has shrunk, or she is growing fatter, and I suspect the latter. When she turns over in her sleep, she rolls out of bed onto the carpet. This has become a regular event most nights during the past couple of weeks.

With a little effort, Carol moved her head to the side. She blinked as she noticed the body lying on the floor next to her.

"That's Barry Jackson. What's wrong with him? Why is he lying on my carpet? What have you done to him?"

"Nothing, he staggered in here and collapsed. Barbara is examining him. Stop talking so much and keep still so I can unwind you."

"Listen, you two," Barbara said in a loud whisper. "People will come to investigate unless we keep the noise down."

"Sorry, Barbara," Carol whispered back. "Dimpy," She turned her head around towards me. "I thought this bed would be okay when I moved here. I meant to get a larger bed and I will soon, I promise."

With another sigh, I began untangling a bedsheet from around a plump, pink leg as we continued to speak in low voices.

"It would be a good idea if we visited the city as soon as possible and bought you a bigger bed."

"Okay," came a muffled voice as I accidentally threw part of the sheet over her head. An extra, extra-large bed, I decided even if it's the only furniture to fit into the room. "Now keep still, and I'll untangle this sheet before it cuts off your circulation."

Pulling the last remaining edge of a sheet from around her, I tossed it onto the bed.

There was a soft yelp from Carol. "Ooh, my head hurts when I move it."

"You must have hit it on the bedside table when you fell onto the carpet. I'll ask Barbara to check you over when she's dealt with Barry."

I changed position to grip her right side. "Now I'm going to roll you onto your back … don't try to help, lie still."

There came plenty of grunts and wheezes, from me, not Carol, as I unwound her from the quilt.

With a bit of help, she clambered onto the bed and straightened her pale blue extra, extra-large nightie over her body. She winced as she ran her fingers through her short, grey curly hair. For a moment, I became fascinated by her rolls of fat swinging to and from elbows to shoulders.

With a shake of the head to stop being mesmerised, I bent and picked up the quilt, which still lay in a jumbled heap on the carpet. After straightening the top sheet across the broad expanse of Carol, I folded and placed the quilt at the foot of the bed then collapsed with a sigh onto a chair. Deep breaths were vital as I waited for my heart rate to return to a reasonable level.

Carol settled back with her head on the pillow. "Thanks for your help, Dimpy, you're an angel, and yes it's become obvious that I need a bigger bed."

She glanced to where Barbara was tending to Barry. "Is Barry going to be all right?"

"I hope so," I looked around to where Barbara was kneeling on the floor. "Now Carol is settled back in her bed, can you tell us what happened to Barry?" I whispered. "Has he had a heart attack?"

Barbara still knelt over him, but as I watched, she sat upright and stretched her back. There was a far-away, sad expression in her eyes as she glanced at me. Through tight lips, her words confirmed my findings. "It is becoming difficult to find a pulse. If the ambulance doesn't arrive soon, he might die." She bent over his body. "But I'll continue with the CPR until they arrive."

Oh, dear. Barry was eighty-one years old and enjoyed giving a vivid description of his insides to anyone who had the misfortune to be passing him in the corridor. What worked and what needed a replacement. Now I come to think of it, most residents of the Manor tried to outdo each other's illness or latest operation. However, now some critical part in Barry's body, perhaps his heart, might have stopped working and killed him.

A familiar sound came from the corridor. Bang, shuffle, shuffle, bang, shuffle, shuffle.

"Emily Barraclough!" Barbara and I both said the same time with a glance towards the open door.

Emily Barraclough, or Mrs B. as we called her, is the Manor's major gossip. She is, without a doubt queen of the stickybeaks. I wondered what had alerted her because she has a unit in a different section to me. The apartment allocated to her has a large living area, complete with a small kitchenette. Although her picture window looks out onto a pretty view of a side garden, this doesn't stop her complaining to people she meets during the day that she needs a patio. In fact, Mrs B whines and moans to everyone, regardless of whether they are staff, residents or visitors.

Those who have lived in the Manor for the longest time have the first choice whenever one of the four patio rooms become vacant. Mrs B is not eligible because she's been a resident at the Manor for just a few months.

The four lucky people with patios are me, Carol, Barry and a good friend of mine, Judith Milner.

I stepped over Barry and walked across to the half-open door. Mrs B, in her green full-length flannelette nightie and a blue plastic cap across the top of large curlers in her grey hair, stood in the doorway. With the cane in her right hand for balance, she peered into Carol's room.

A murmur of voices floated along the corridor from the front entrance to the Manor. The ambulance had arrived, and Mrs B was forgotten in my haste to unlock the Manor front door for the paramedics. They grabbed their equipment, followed me back to Carol's room and hurried inside.

# Chapter 3

Bang, shuffle, shuffle, bang, shuffle, shuffle.

Mrs B!

Eyes now open, I could hear a heavy walking stick making an extra loud noise outside my apartment.

I groaned. Emily Barraclough, the Manors noisy and nosy early bird. You would expect all the excitement during the night to have tired her out. Her mind must have been at a boiling point, wondering what had happened as she stood in the doorway of Carol's room. Why was the manager involved? Had Carol fallen out of bed again? Also, why was Barry lying on the carpet?

Mrs B's appearance in the corridor last night had been forgotten in haste to put Barry into the ambulance and rushed to the hospital.

Two hours later, after the ambulance left the Manor; Barbara received a mobile call from an intensive care nurse at the hospital. Despite all attempts to save him, Barry had passed away.

Although it was after three o'clock in the morning, I was still awake when she tapped on my door and told me the sad news.

As a consequence, with everything that happened during the night and Barbara's news about Barry's death, I tossed and turned for another hour before managing to fall sleep. Memories of Barry lying on the carpet kept flooding into my mind along with visions of Carol as a giant whale struggling in a bed of seaweed.

With a yawn, I slipped out of bed and donned my dressing gown and slippers before creeping over to the door and opening it wide enough to peek out. Mrs B, cane in hand, stood there ready to knock again.

There was no *Good morning, Dimpy. How are you?* Instead, words oozed from her lips like treacle. "Is Barry dead? Does this mean I'll be able to move into his apartment because he won't need it any longer?" She shook her cane in my face. "As I've tried to explain ever since I arrived here, I should have the best accommodation in the Manor." She banged the cane onto the floor. "Which means not stuck in a dump of a room without space to put personal items on show, or a patio to relax on." The cane waved in front of my face again. "I deserve better."

I pushed the cane aside and opened my mouth to get a word in edgeways, but without stopping for breath, Mrs B continued. "I am a well-respected member of society and used to the best of everything. So …"

For heaven's sakes, surely she didn't expect me to reply to her inane grumbles. Not to mention having to listen to her whiny voice first thing in the morning. Still tired and depressed from the news of Barry's death, and without a shred of sympathy or a word of goodbye, I closed the door on her and returned to bed.

After a few minutes, the sound of the cane diminished as Mrs B plodded away from the door. Now I was wide awake; it would be useless going back to sleep. Instead, I relaxed, made myself comfortable on a recliner and started to read a magazine; something to help pass the time until I dressed for breakfast.

But I'm getting a wee bit ahead of myself.

My name is Margaret Gruar – middle name Anastasia – but I

don't advertise the fact. Most people call me Dimpy, which I prefer. When I smile, two big dimples appear on each side of my face – large dimples. I've had them ever since I was a little girl.

For many years I worked as a Reference Librarian and Archivist at a University. On retiring, my husband and I moved back to Tasmania, where I had spent my childhood. After David died, all my time went into writing novels. Using the pseudonym Gayle Lovejoy, I've had four novellas and eBooks published by a well-known romance publishing company. Number Five has been commissioned and is due for publication in two months. Or at least that is when the publisher wants the finished manuscript on his desk.

I rattled around a big old house in Hobart, becoming more and more lonely. My married daughter suggested I move into a one-bedroom bungalow at the rear of their noisy, busy family home in Queensland.

After thinking it over for two minutes, I realised this would not work. Peace and quiet were essential while I wrote my novellas, and I needed to be close to my agent in Melbourne. I loved my family but found a two-week holiday each year with them was enough. The hot and sometimes humid weather did not agree with me and, besides, I love my life in Tasmania.

I began searching in earnest for a place I could call home, and after a few months found the perfect spot. I sold the house and moved into the Mountain View Residential Manor in Kinross, a small town in the north of Tasmania with views of the Great Western Tiers in the background.

At seventy-seven years of age, all my faculties still seem to be okay, due in part to the fact solving crosswords and walking are favourite activities. I hope to continue to old age – a hundred would be a nice round figure. A congratulations letter from the Queen, (or King) and one from the Prime Minister would look great on the cabinet next to the television.

One minor problem remains. Six feet tall, skinny as a matchstick with large feet, I have a habit of tripping over things when they are below my eye level.

Bang, shuffle, shuffle, bang, shuffle, shuffle. The sound of a cane came again – Mrs B's hobble.

It's time the Board of Management invested in carpet instead of the blue linoleum in the corridors I thought, as I released the recliner and stood up. Something soft with a deep pile to muffle Mrs B's cane.

After listening for a knock, I sighed with relief. Mrs B wasn't after me this time; instead, her footsteps and cane passed by without stopping. No doubt heading for the dining room, where, as usual, she would set herself up before the early breakfast arrivals trickled in. It had become a ritual with her, to sit beside the door and tick each person's name in an exercise book as they entered the dining room.

Mrs B always wore a dark blue, brown or black plain twinset with a single strand of pearls and a blue, green or red tartan skirt. Thick stockings and sensible brown or black lace-up shoes completed the outfit. She hobbles along the corridor with the help of her cane, which bangs onto the floor at every third step.

It has an instant effect. As soon as the sound of the cane comes towards them, even deaf people scatter. They either disappear through the nearest exit or pretend to be in a hurry to go somewhere else. I think I have already mentioned she is not the most popular person in the Manor.

She is the grimmest, long-faced, frosty, most bad-tempered old lady in the world. As far as I remember, she has never said a kind word about anyone except her family. They, according to her, are God's gift to humankind.

One day while passing by, the door to her room stood open. Nobody else was in the corridor, so I took a quick peek into the unit. Posed photos of herself at different ages were hanging on the walls – not a family group photo in sight. A few photographs of a grim-faced young man hung high on the wall behind her bed. One photo showed him as a young child, the other as an older lad, possibly in his forties. He reminded me of a male version of Mrs B., so I assumed it must be her son.

However, no resident at the Manor has ever met anyone from her family in the flesh. Oh, yes, I did once. I happened to see him a few weeks ago when we almost collided outside the manager's office. I guessed the sour look on the son's face, and the scowl on Mrs B's meant there must have been an argument with Barbara. Not to their advantage, I thought. At any rate, the son resembled his photo. He was a short, skinny fellow with pitch-black hair, thin pointy face and a big nose, similar to his mother. He ignored me, muttered a few words to her, threw his arms in the air and strode towards the exit. Mrs B hobbled along next to him, banging and shuffling her cane on the linoleum floor. He slammed the entrance door open, and just about knocked his mother over as he strode past her and clumped down the steps without turning back to say goodbye.

I checked my wristwatch. There was no time left for reminiscing; it was after eight o'clock. I needed to get a move on. Breakfast was served in the dining room between 7.30 am and 9.30 am. Mrs B ticked our names when we arrived for breakfast, but not for lunch or dinner. Why? No one knew. When asked, she said it benefitted the staff and refused to answer any more questions.

I put those thoughts to one side, changed out of my nightdress and donned a dark green pleated skirt and light mauve V-necked jumper. My short silver-grey hair needed a brush, or it clumps in untidy curls. I checked my appearance in a mirror to make sure my panties had not pushed up over the back of my skirt. The final touch was a dab of lipstick before I hurried into the corridor and made my way to the dining room.

# Chapter 4

At twenty-five past eight, I strolled into the dining room, nodded good morning to Mrs B and watched as she scrolled a finger down her list. She found my name, licked the tip of the pencil, gave it a tick then glared in my direction as I walked past her into the room.

Each of the eight tables in the dining room seat six people and were covered with blue and white gingham tablecloths. They were set for breakfast with knife, fork and spoon settings, and side plates. A silver rack, ready to fill with hot toast sat in the middle of each table along with a small vase of flowers and foliage from the Manor gardens.

Painted light green, the walls of the dining room, as with all the public rooms and corridors in the Manor displayed paintings by local artists and were a mixture of seascapes, views of the town, the river and the Great Western Tiers mountain range.

The room was near capacity this morning, but I was sure my usual breakfast companions would have kept a seat for me at their table. I nodded to residents eating their breakfast as I passed them on my way to the buffet bench set up near the kitchen at the far end of the room. As usual, there were several items to choose from – bacon, eggs, tomatoes, porridge, cereals and fresh fruit, to name a few. They fed us well at the

Manor. An urn steamed away on a separate table. Containers marked coffee, Milo, tea and sugar stood in a row. Two jugs of fresh milk, one labelled full cream, the other skim, sat behind them. Teaspoons sat in a box next to a small flip-top rubbish bin. On the lid, printed in large black letters, a sign read *used teabags only*.

While pondering the health benefits of a hearty breakfast, I spotted Carol ahead of me in the queue, a large bruise above her eye prominent on the right side of her head. Barbara had checked her for concussion while the paramedics worked on Barry because it could account for the strange behaviour after her fall. One of the ambos also gave her another quick check after they loaded Barry into the ambulance. Barbara promised the paramedics to monitor her during the night in case there were problems. She would ring for the ambulance if they needed to return and take Carol to the hospital.

The bump to her head didn't seem to have taken away her appetite. Her tray was piled high with large amounts of eggs, bacon, sausages, tomatoes and two small packets of cornflakes. I asked if her head was still sore from her night-time fall and gave her a *that's good* smile when she told me she was okay, and her head was not as painful this morning.

The cooks, Rita and Daisy, were visible through the open kitchen door. Daisy raised a hand, nodded and smiled hello. Rita took no notice, busy pounding something with a wooden mallet.

The two ladies are nice enough, but temperament wise they're poles apart. Daisy, the short, round one, laughs and kids around with the residents and the rest of the staff. Like a busy bee, she flits around the place on the lookout for things to empty, dust or clean. I watched as she put the used dishes into a dishwasher then loaded trays ready to top up the toast racks.

Rita is the exact opposite of Daisy. Tall and thin with never a smile, she keeps to herself. She's a capable, earnest worker, although something of an enigma – always long-faced as if something terrible is about to happen.

During the week, Rita and Daisy cook the main meals and make sandwiches and slices. A temporary cook comes in during the weekends. We always have tuna or salmon mornay on Saturdays and either chicken, beef or pork roast on Sundays. Vegans and vegetarians seem to be in short supply at the Manor. However, I'm sure Rita and Daisy are capable of attending to any special dietary needs.

Not being a lover of hot breakfasts, I picked up a tray and loaded it with a small packet of cereal, a jug of milk and pats of butter for the toast.

My friends Judith Milner and Ronni Goodman waved me to the table where they sat near a window. I left Rita and Daisy to their own business. With care not to trip over feet or chairs, I held the loaded tray in both hands and weaved between the tables. They grinned at me when I arrived and placed my tray in front of an empty seat.

Judith is eighty-three years old with natural blue-grey curly hair. With a tiny figure, she loves clothes with big flowers on them or plain bright colours. Aqua, teal, magenta and orange are favourites. This morning's dress was bright red splattered with pink roses.

After I put my tray on the table and sat, she leaned forward towards me. In a low voice, she said, "We saw you wave to Daisy and Rita. Did Rita crack a smile? We made a bet. I said nobody gets a smile from her. Who was right?"

I shook my head and chuckled. This was typical behaviour of them as they tried to evoke a sense of humour into a situation. "You win, Judith. No smile but be careful. If OB Jolly – (their nickname for Rita) – finds out you make fun of her behind her back, there's no telling what she might do. Perhaps drop the odd cockroach in your food."

"I wonder how her daughter is?" Judith said. "Rita used to mention Florence sometimes. Not nowadays, though."

"There's gossip around," Ronni said. "Somebody mentioned she's getting married."

Eyes serious, she turned her attention towards me. "Are you okay, Dimpy? You seem hung-over. Perhaps you have been nipping too much from the whiskey bottle of yours?"

"I'm fine," I said. "Just tired from lack of sleep last night."

Although her birth certificate says her name is Veronica Petunia Goodman, she only answers to Ronni. Seventy-nine years of age and skinny as a rake, she wears her clothes like a model which was her past vocation. An old model now, but with her figure, she would look good wearing a sack. She still dresses in stylish clothes and struts around like a bantam rooster. Most of the residents enjoy the occasional impromptu parade. Nobody laughs or ridicules her.

Today she wore a well-cut grey pants suit with a pink lacy camisole and a pair of highly polished low-heeled black shoes. With her salon streaked grey and white hair shaped into a pageboy, and a touch of makeup to her heart-shaped face, she was a picture of elegance.

While unloading my tray, I explained how, once again, Carol fell out of bed during the night.

"There she lay, head on the floor, legs spread up onto the side of the bed and her nightie around her neck. This time she hit her head on the bedside table before landing on the carpet."

"Something needs to be done about her," Ronni said. "She can't sleep in a single bed anymore; she's too fat. You will strain the muscles in your back if you continue lifting her weight much longer."

"Being on the other side of you, and a sound sleeper, I never hear Carol fall," Judith said. "Or I would help you get her back into bed."

"Thanks for the thought, but soon I may not need any help. She has asked me to accompany her to the city to buy a double bed."

Tears formed. How did I tell my best friends about Barry?

Judith gave me an intent look. "Did something else happen last night we need to know about?"

"Yes."

They gave me their full attention as I continued in a low, sad voice, "Barry Jackson staggered into Carol' apartment and had a funny turn. He fell onto the carpet, gurgled and almost died right in front of me."

There was a gasp from Judith. "How awful," she said. "Was the ambulance called? Is he in the hospital? Did they manage to save him?"

"No, Judith, I'm afraid not. Barbara told me the terrible news early this morning. Although the paramedics tried all they could to keep him alive, Barry died in the ambulance on the way to the hospital."

Silence.

Judith stared at me, porridge tipping off the spoon held to her mouth.

"Time for a cup of tea," I rose to my feet and placed my napkin on the table.

While I made my drink, it gave me a chance to organise my thoughts. With the facts sorted in my mind, I re-joined them. After a swallow of tea, it was time to explain what had occurred during the night. They both listened with rapt attention as I sipped my drink and told them in greater detail how Barry had burst into Carol's room. I explained how Barbara tried to save his life with CPR and about his unexpected death.

I buttered my toast and described how Mrs B arrived on the scene and poked her nose into the room in an attempt to find out what had happened

"So, ladies, there has been no nip of whiskey. As for the

hung-over look, my excuse is I was awake until the early hours while I dealt with Carol, Barry, and the delightful Mrs B."

Breakfast eaten; I made another cup of tea. Both ladies were still pensive when I resumed my seat at the table. Judith was the first to recover, but her mouth opened and closed as she struggled to find what to say. The words refused to come out. Ronni blinked as she returned to the present, looked at Judith, and spoke for her. "The question is, why did Barry die so quickly and in such an undignified manner?"

"Yes," Judith said, as she pushed the chair back and rose to her feet. "Barry was our friend. He was as fit as a fiddle when I spoke to him yesterday afternoon. I cannot believe he's dead."

By this time, her voice had risen to a shout. A few of the other diners, who found this sudden interlude of more interest than their breakfast, stopped eating and turned in their seats to watch us.

"Why?" Judith persisted, leaning over the table towards me, her voice even louder now. "Tell us! What happened to Barry?"

"Steady on," I said. "Don't get into a tizzy. Sit back in your chair and try to stay calm."

"Yes," Ronni chimed in. "Perhaps a few deep breaths would help."

Judith was prone to get distraught when she didn't understand what happened around her. A few weeks earlier, her daughter, Dianne, accompanied her to an appointment with a specialist at the Launceston hospital who was an expert in different types of dementia. On their return, Dianne told Ronni and me the diagnosis showed her mother had Fronto Temporal Lobar Degeneration. This disease would continue to worsen as there was no cure. Day by day, her personality began a slow change before our eyes. Ronni and I, along with her other friends, tried to ignore the symptoms and continued to treat her in the same way we acted towards each other.

A sob escaped as she lowered herself onto her chair and fumbled in a pocket for a tissue.

"Sorry, Judith," I said. "At the moment, there is no reason for Barry's sudden death, but there will be an autopsy. As soon as I learn anything about what happened to him, I'll let you know."

Satisfied, she wiped her eyes and sank back into her chair, picked up her cup and drank her tea. The rest of the diners turned around to finish their breakfast. Having heard Judith's outburst, they discussed Barry's death in low tones. The excitement was over.

Judith spoke in a reflective voice. "It's so sad when someone you know dies, especially when they are a friend."

Ronni nodded. "Mrs B won't be upset because she crosses people off her list when they die. A chance to dress up and attend funerals is something she enjoys doing."

We sat in stillness for a while reflecting on what had happened to Barry.

Ronni broke the silence. "How is Carol after her tumble out of bed last night? Have you seen her this morning?"

I nodded and pointed to where she sat at a table near the door, having an animated conversation with her breakfast companions. No doubt she would tell them with lots of embellishments about her fall and what happened to Barry. Her hands waved in the air for emphasis.

"Did he have any relatives?" Judith asked. "His wife died ten years ago from cancer. There were no children, and he never mentioned other family members when we talked together."

Because it was obvious who *he* was, I answered: "Barbara told the paramedics she would give the hospital any information the Manor has on file about relatives. They will contact the next of kin."

"We'll find out who they are when the funeral arrangements are announced," Ronni replied.

Nobody felt like talking anymore, so we sat and sipped our drinks in silent thought.

# Chapter 5

At twenty past nine, Don Ahegge, whose surname sounded like a Russian cough, breezed through the dining-room door. Most days, he would be the last person to arrive for breakfast.

This time before she ticked his name off the list, Mrs B stood up and lifted her wristwatch until it almost touched Don's nose. Her face scrunched up until it looked like a squashed piece of fruit. She tapped the dial with her index finger and opened her mouth to speak. Don took no notice of her antics. He placed his finger on his lips and shook his head, then laughed.

"It's not friggin' 9.30 yet darlin', so tick me off, there's a good girl."

Hands on hips, a scowl on her face, Mrs B glared at him as he walked past her into the room.

After a great show of ticking his name, Mrs B closed her book and put it and the pencil she had been using into her handbag. We all must have been present and correct – except for Barry. She stood and shouldered her way past Don to the buffet to select her choices for breakfast. When she had her tray full of food, she made a beeline to where Carol sat, hoping to hear the latest gossip about Barry's death.

As Don crossed the dining room floor behind her, he waved and nodded to friends as he passed their tables. Although his lousy language could be a problem, most people tolerated him for the way he took an interest in them. H listened to their stories and difficulties—everybody except Mrs B.

Just after she arrived at the Manor, he told me Mrs B didn't like him because he called her a stupid frigging bitch and should get a life.

Don waited until she left the buffet, helped himself to a tray and loaded it with what remained of the bacon, tomato and egg, then walked to the urn and made a coffee.

Always clean-shaven, with a round face, blue eyes thick, grey eyebrows and a ready smile, Don is the typical Aussie male. He would have been good looking when he was young, but at eighty-two, he had run to fat, and his huge belly hung over the top of his shorts. Summer or winter he always wore a pair of khaki shorts with a blue, red or green striped tee shirt. Grey ankle socks poked out from his sandals.

With his tray balanced in his hands, he sauntered over to our table. "G'day girls," he said as he sat in a chair and helped himself to a piece of toast. "What 's up? Why the long faces? Have you killed a friggin' cat?"

"Eat your breakfast," I said, "while I tell you what happened last night."

"Well, I'll be a friggin' bandicoot," he said after he heard the news. "So poor old Barry's carked it. Whatta way to go, takin' his last breath on the floor next to Carol." He grinned and continued, "Mind you; I wouldn't mind lyin' next to her – not dead, of course. Just lyin' there. Maybe I'd be able to solve a few mysteries, like if she wore those massive knickers of hers under her nightie. I've seen 'em dryin' on the clothesline; they're friggin' beauties. Reminds me of sails on a ship they do."

"Don," I said, "don't be so disrespectful. It's not nice to link Barry's death with Carol's knickers."

A glance around the table had my face turn red with

embarrassment. It was apparent I had made matters worse. There were grins on their faces. All the same, Don wasn't far off the mark. Her knickers *were* massive; each pair took up four times more room on the clothesline than anybody else's underwear.

It was time for me to leave. "See you later for coffee in the rec room," I said with a nod to everyone and took my used dishes and tray back to the kitchen. Ronni and Judith decided to stay and chat with Don while he finished his breakfast.

My room beckoned. Some peace would be welcome, and time was needed to come to terms with Barry's sad and sudden death.

Although the Manor employs someone to do the vacuuming, dusting and washing the floor of the kitchenettes, I prefer to tidy the rooms myself.

My apartment consists of a large bedroom with built-in cupboards, combined with a small lounge area big enough for my recliner and coffee table. A small rolltop desk and office chair just fitted into a corner. My combined television/DVD player sits on a two-door blackwood chiffonier which is against on the wall facing the bed. I picked up the photo of my parents that sat on the coffee table. There was no memory of my father because he died from lung cancer not long after I was born. My mother told me the gory details the first time she caught me as a teenager with a cigarette in my mouth. It should have been enough to put me off smoking for life, but I still enjoyed the occasional puff.

My mother contracted Parkinson's disease while I was a teenager at high school. With the help of a part-time carer, I looked after her until she died on my twentieth birthday. After her death, I enrolled to do a postgraduate qualification in library and information studies.

The other photo was a favourite and showed my husband, David, with our German Shepherd, Digger, perched on a rock fishing. Or I should say, David was fishing. Digger, who loved to eat fish, sat waiting for some trout to be caught, and become his dinner.

The apartment also had a small kitchenette with a cupboard for crockery and glasses, microwave oven, and electric jug. Last year I added a one cup coffee machine. The ensuite has enough room in the shower for a bath chair. A toilet sat in a corner furthest from the door. A basin with a mirror and a cupboard underneath for storing towels and spare toiletries stood opposite the toilet.

The best part of my apartment is the patio. Double glass doors lead out onto the covered area, of a reasonable depth with steps leading to the lawn at the rear of the Manor. It runs along the whole back part of the unit. A small wrought iron table stands in the corner closest to the doors, complete with two comfortable outdoor chairs. Matching wrought iron pot-plant holders, two shelves high, sit either end of the patio. Sometimes I forget to water them. However, we are blessed by the fact that Tasmania has a good rainfall, or my plants might never survive.

I made the bed, straightened my library books on the bedside table and unfolded the three-part screen, with beautiful scenes of waterfalls and birds, brought back from a trip to Japan many years ago. It is perfect as a divider between my bed area and the rest of the room.

In a flurry of activity, cupboards were checked in case more supplies were required. My single malt whiskey bottle was low. It would need replacing soon. As my friends were aware, I enjoyed a wee nip of an evening or occasionally during the late afternoon.

I swept the tiny kitchenette, wiped the top of the bench and checked a small cupboard which contained crockery, teabags in a glass jar and a packet of coffee pods for my machine. Under the counter was a small refrigerator, and I noted in my memory to acquire more milk and cheese from the Manor kitchen. Also, another packet of dry biscuits would not go amiss.

In the ensuite, I washed my hands and brushed my hair. When I moved into the Manor, it had been great to find the mirror in the bathroom was high enough to see myself without having to crouch. While in there I wiped the shower screen with paper towelling, put used towels in the laundry basket, and arranged two clean ones on the rail next to the toilet. I like to have my shower before going to bed.

Housework finished, it was time to visit the recreation area, known as the rec room, for a coffee with my friends.

# Chapter 6

Apart from the coffee machine on a table near the window, the rec room has an extensive four-shelf bookcase library, and a magazine rack full of used periodicals and daily newspapers. A large television screen sits in a corner, with comfy seats and room for wheelchairs.

Headphones are left on a low table in easy reach, and residents are asked to use them when watching the TV. This way, the sound does not annoy other people using the room for different purposes.

A large uncarpeted area in the middle of the room is kept clear for dances, visiting entertainers and exercise classes. Activities such as art classes, guitar lessons and drama groups also use the room during the week.

The rec room was an ideal place to pick up snippets of gossip as most of the residents spent time here during the day. I'd poke around and kept my ears open for any talk about Barry. For some unknown reason, there was a niggle in my mind, which meant I disagreed that he died from natural causes.

As I walked along the corridor, I spotted Rita and Barbara talking as they stood close together outside the door to the rec room. Still chatting, they entered and crossed to the coffee unit near the picture windows with a view of the garden and distant hills.

I wondered if they were discussing Barry. There was nobody else in the room, but I worried they would spot me as I attempted to eavesdrop on their conversation. Like a shadow, I sneaked into the room. Hoping not to be seen, I stood beside by the TV set and bookcase, which almost overflowed with romance and murder mystery paperbacks. I pretended to read the titles. Some copies of my books were on the middle shelf.

As soon as Barbara and Rita made their drinks, they moved to the window and stared out at the view of the Great Western Tiers. Meanwhile, I moved closer to the table holding the coffee-making unit.

They had their backs turned towards the machine as they sipped their drinks. Their voices drifted back to where I stood. Confident they could not see me, I crept closer to them.

"Did Barry have any relatives?" Rita said.

"As far as I can remember, no family members have visited him since he arrived at the Manor. However, I think there is the name of a relative in his file. I'll look it up as soon as I return to the office. The police and the hospital will need to know his name and phone number. They'll contact him with the information that Barry has passed away."

"Why were the police called in?" Rita said.

I pricked up my ears at this piece of information.

"I don't know for sure," Barbara replied. "According to the hospital, a doctor suspects Barry may have been poisoned. They are continuing with more tests. I assume this is the reason the police are involved."

"Bother the police!" Rita exclaimed. "I bet the first thing they'll want do is check his tablets to see if the staff make a mistake. You don't think they have, do you?"

"No, we always make sure the dosage is correct. It's a necessary procedure. We also train the staff to keep an eye on the residents when giving out their medications.

"Anyway, to cut a long story short, the police said they would be here this afternoon to make enquiries."

Then the worst imaginable thing happened. To hear better, I leaned over too far, stumbled, almost fell and cracked my left elbow on the edge of the coffee unit.

"Oof," I said as I scrambled to my feet.

There was a pause as Rita and Barbara stopped talking, spun around and stared at me. Feeling foolish, I tried to mumble apologies and brush myself down. Then, not sure what to say or do, I mumbled an "excuse me, things to do" and hurried to the door. As I left the room, I sensed their eyes boring into my back.

# Chapter 7

In the corridor, I stopped for a moment to catch my breath. Then I realised how stupid I'd been. Barbara was my friend, Rita, a friendly acquaintance. Instead of being so idiotic, a casual approach after the fall, perhaps a *'G'day, how's it going'*, would have been better. Then I would not have acted like a guilty child caught with her hand in the cookie jar. When our paths crossed again, I would try to correct matters. Right now, it would be an excellent time to retreat to my room.

Once there, I opened the desk and fired up the laptop computer. Not much of interest, except for an email from the publisher asking when my next manuscript would be ready. The story was half-finished, but Brenda's fate at the hands of the irresistible stranger would have to wait. It would be difficult to focus on a romantic novella while Barry's death was on my mind.

My thoughts turned to what Barbara and Rita had been discussing. Barry's medication. Barbara was strict about everybody's medicine. However, the unexpected way Barry had died seemed unusual. I decided to dismiss thoughts about his death from my mind. It would be better to wait until the police and the doctor had made their conclusions about whether he had been poisoned or died from natural causes.

I switched the laptop off and stretched my shoulders and back. The rec room beckoned again. My friends might be there now. It would be nice to have coffee and chat about everyday things. Anything that would take my mind off thoughts that Barry might have been murdered

The daily exercise class was in action as I walked into the rec room—one of the many activities on offer to keep us oldies occupied. A mixed group of men and women were performing seated exercises. At the instructor's command, they waved their arms and legs in time with the loud music. The one, two, three, stretch thing was not my idea of fun. Pictures of demented robots flashed through my mind.

Over in a corner, Carol sat with a group of women. It was apparent she was telling a rapt audience her version of the events during the night. A smile crept onto my face. The story would become longer and more detailed each time she told someone. By now she would have attempted to save Barry while Barbara and I stood by and watched in admiration.

I made my way past them to join Judith, Ronni and Don where they sat in comfortable recliner armchairs facing the large picture window. The view from here never failed to relax me as I looked out over the Great Western Tiers. Today a thin line of snow ran along the tops with large grey snow clouds banking up behind.

Don disturbed my reveries. "Sit back Dimpy, take the weight off your brains." he said, "Tell us the latest friggin' info. About Barry, I mean."

Once seated, I raised my voice over the loud music to tell them I overheard Barbara mention to Rita that the police would visit the Manor later today. "They want to check Barry's medication," I told them.

A mobile phone rang. "Someone's in strife," Judith said. "They're always told to turn off their phones during the exercise class. It's a strict rule." The trainer switched off the music. The phone kept ringing as the exercisers sorted through their discarded clothes and other items such as handbags, anywhere a mobile could hide.

"I've found it," a voice from the front of the group called out. I chuckled to myself as the instructor withdrew her mobile phone from her handbag. She turned it off, placed it back in her bag and apologised for the disruption. The class came back to order, and the exercises resumed.

"If the friggin police are comin'," Don said, "they'll want to interview us, so we'd better get our friggin stories straight."

"What stories?" Ronni said, in an indignant voice. "I slept right through it, so I don't need one."

"You never know, we might," Don said, "We don't want to look friggin guilty of anythin'."

"Don't be silly," I said. "Cover stories aren't needed. Barry died in unusual circumstances. As a result, the doctor at the hospital is unhappy about the results. This is the reason why the police were brought into the picture."

"Friggin hell! I don't like it. Not at all. The bit about the police, I mean. Are you sure they won't want to talk to me? Not that I'm friggin worried or anything, just uncomfortable around 'em."

"Nothing for you to concern yourself about," I reassured him. "You weren't there when he died. They will interview Barbara about Barry's medication. Barbara and Rita talked about them earlier, because the police would be interested in knowing how many tablets Barry took each day." I stopped to take a deep breath, then took a sip of coffee. "So, no, Don, you don't have to worry. However, it would be helpful if you keep your eyes and ears open. You're good at picking up stray bits of gossip. I have a niggling suspicion the police are right, and Barry's death wasn't natural. It was too sudden."

Don added, "Also friggin' unexpected."

The constant loud beat of the music was getting on my nerves. "I'll see you guys at lunch for an update. I'm going for a walk to get a much-needed breath of fresh air."

"Hey!" Don said as I got up from the chair, "watch who your friggin' trippin' over."

"Sorry, It's these big feet of mine. They're always in the way."

I said my goodbyes and hurried back to my apartment. I hated to tread on people's toes.

# Chapter 8

Right now seemed a good idea for a walk to my favourite hideaway. I fetched a warm jacket from my built-in double wardrobe set into the wall next to my bed before going across to the patio door. It was late winter and still cold.

Shrugging into the jacket, I stepped outside onto a strip of lawn that borders my flagstone patio. From here, a short dirt path winds through the bushes to a clearing hidden from the building.

When I first moved into my apartment, I noticed there was no fence between the end of the lawn and a patch of scrub between the Manor and a side road.

With time to explore, I wandered along an overgrown path, delighted to find it led to a small clearing among the bushes where an ancient eucalyptus tree had fallen over. The log proved a handy place to sit, although, with my height and creaky old knees, I had to be careful when squatting in case my balance went out of kilter and landed me on the ground.

Because I like the occasional cigarette, and smoking is forbidden anywhere in the Manor building and grounds, this secluded area suited me fine. Complete with a log to sit on and nobody to complain that a cigarette is bad for you because you will die of cancer.

Perched on the log, I dug my fingers into the hollow and felt around for a Zip-loc bag, then reached in a little farther to draw out a small round covered ashtray. I put them on the log next to me, took a cigarette and lighter from the plastic bag, lit up and relaxed. While taking puffs, I listened to the birds – mostly wrens and the starlings with the occasional warble of a blackbird – while thoughts of Barry crept into my head. His death had been so sudden. Was it an overdose of his medication? Perhaps a recently discovered rare disease. A severe shock. Or a sudden heart attack.

Maybe the sight of Carol as she lay on the carpet among a bundle of sheets, was enough to give anybody a shock. *Behave yourself, I thought. Don't be ridiculous.*

My mind turned to foul play. Did someone in the Manor kill Barry?

Unbelievable. Because he seemed harmless enough. Now and then he occasionally wandered uninvited into people's rooms. Although from forgetfulness or accidentally on purpose, we weren't sure. Whatever it was, we didn't care. Most of us had peculiarities of one type or another. Barry would have been no different. Instead, we had laughed and dismissed his oddball habits.

Equally important, a few people might not have found Barry's unusual behaviour funny. Perhaps they considered it a little too upsetting in their last years when all they wanted was peace and quiet. However, it seemed ridiculous to believe he was murdered because he annoyed someone. Or had a crush on a lady and got rebuffed. A chuckle escaped me. Barry might have received a slap on the face, but murder ... no.

None of the reasons I could think of made much sense. Don't be silly; I scolded myself. Perhaps the doctors are wrong, and it was a heart attack. While the paramedics were working on Barry before loading him into the ambulance, I had asked them what they thought had happened.

"It appears to be a heart attack," was the reply, "The doctor will make a proper diagnosis once we get him to the hospital."

I gave a quiet laugh. This would make a good plot for a murder mystery. A pity my paperbacks were about romance and not homicide.

A glance at my watch showed it was ten minutes to twelve, almost lunchtime. I stubbed out my cigarette in the ashtray, replaced everything into the plastic bag and tucked it into the hollow log.

I stood up and brushed bark chips from my skirt, ready to return to the Manor – and froze.

A rustle had come from behind me, followed by a noise inside the hollow log. A snake? Reptiles like hollow logs. *Hang on Dimpy, I told myself, don't panic.* I tried to remember anything I had read about what to do when being faced with a snake in the bush. Back in time, I'd been told never to run or make any sudden movements. Stand still like a tree and don't, under any circumstances, try to do it any harm. Otherwise, the snake will strike and bite you, after which, you might die.

A memory surfaced about placing my hand into the hollow log to reach the cigarettes, and my heart did the quickstep.

In case whatever caused the noise showed itself and became angry, I backed off from the log one slow step at a time. This seemed a sensible thing to do because a long-forgotten fact, I had read somewhere, also flashed into my mind. *All snakes in Tasmania are poisonous.*

Then a head appeared from the hollow in the log. A tiny hairy face with a startled expression peeped out at me. Not a snake, they don't have furry faces. My visitor, who had almost given me heart failure, was a harmless bandicoot. Without warning, it shot out of the log and disappeared into the bushes.

As a result of the fright, my body shook, and it took ten deep breathes before the tremors were under control.

When my heartbeat slowed to an almost normal rhythm, I walked back to the patio – all worries about Barry's death replaced by the sight of a pint-sized, defenceless marsupial.

## Chapter 9

Back in my apartment, I removed the jacket and stood in the ensuite to brush my hair and had a general tidy. When I was satisfied with my appearance, I collected my handbag and opened the door. My stomach began to grumble as a rich aroma wafted along the corridor. A reminder that today was Casserole Wednesday.

At the buffet table, I dished up a plate of beef stew loaded with vegetables and dumplings. After buttering a piece of wholemeal bread, I carried my tray over to join Ronni, where she sat alone at a table close to the kitchen. On my way, I spotted Mrs B eating lunch near the entrance to the dining room. Being ticked off on her list occurred only at breakfast time.

Mrs B usually ate meals alone because nobody wanted to sit with her. Her nasty attitude towards everyone meant they believed she brought it on herself with her permanent scowl and bad temper. A pleasant conversation would be awkward with her grumpy mood to take into consideration.

Ronni smiled and nodded hello as I pulled up a chair and sat opposite her. "Pleased you could join me, Dimpy, I dislike eating alone. Don's gone out to have steak and chips with his mates at the local pub," she said when I glanced at the empty chairs at the table. "Don told me he'd eaten enough casseroles to last him a friggin' lifetime. His words, not mine – and before you ask, I have no idea where Judith is."

"Don must be mad. The casseroles are fine; they always taste good." My gaze wandered around the room. "I wonder where she is. Judith, I mean. It's not like her to miss a meal. Perhaps she has forgotten it was lunchtime. Nowadays, her head's a real scatterbrain at times."

Ronni shrugged. "Her dementia seems worse, and I haven't seen her since morning tea in the rec room. She was going back to her apartment for a rest and to read a new copy of her favourite magazine until lunchtime."

"If she is not here in the next ten minutes, I'll knock on her door and make sure she's okay," I said, with a look at my watch.

Ronni let out a sharp squeal and stared at something over my right shoulder. "No need to do that, I can see her now," she said. "All too clearly, in fact."

Because my back faced towards the door, I swivelled around to see where Ronni was looking. Instead of the usual clatter, the dining room had become quiet. Everyone stopped eating as they, too, stared open-mouthed at the tiny figure framed in the doorway.

The sudden hush caused Daisy and Rita to leave off what they were doing and poke their heads out the kitchen door to find out why there was a sudden silence.

Judith stood in the doorway dressed in a semi-transparent knee-length pink nightie, which did not leave much to the imagination. A sigh of relief escaped my lips. Thank goodness Don wasn't here. He would have laughed or made an outrageous remark.

Judith's slippers click-clacked on the linoleum as she made her way over to our table. "Why is it so quiet in here? Am I too late?" she asked when she reached us. "For lunch, I mean."

"Never mind about being late," Ronni said, with a stunned look. "Why are you wearing a negligee?"

"Wha—what do you mean? I changed into a tracksuit and lay down on my bed for my nap after morning tea. When I realised it was twelve-thirty and the kitchen staff would have started dishing up our meals, I put my clothes back on and hurried straight here."

Ronni nodded in the general direction of Judith's dress choice for the day, which brought a quick response.

"Oh dear," Judith said with a tremble in her voice as she lowered her eyes and saw what she wore. "This can't be right?" Tears welled up in her eyes. "I don't know why I'm wearing my nightie instead of a dress."

"Don't worry," I said, hugging her. "We'll go back to your apartment and start again. Rita and Daisy will not mind if you're a few minutes late." I glared around the room and added in a louder voice, "Everybody in here will mind their own business, won't they?"

Without looking to see if they had heard, I stood and nodded to Ronni. "We'll be back in about fifteen minutes."

"Would you like me to ask Daisy to keep your meals warm until you return?" Ronni asked.

"Yes, please. Come along, Judith."

As we left, the noise of people eating, and chatting began again.

We toddled along the corridor to Judith's apartment, three doors along the hall from mine. I sat on an armchair and waited as she changed into a blue and white striped skirt and purple jumper which lay on the doona. It did not take a genius to guess these were the clothes she was supposed to wear for lunch.

"Why would I have put my nightie on?" Her voice was little more than a squeak. "These are the clothes I meant to wear. That's why they're on the bed."

"Your mind could have still been fuzzy when you woke from your nap. No harms been done, Judith, so when you're ready, we'll head back to the dining room."

"Okay. I'll get changed while you wait." Judith took her skirt and jumper into the bathroom and brushed her hair before she came back out, fully dressed.

"Right you are then, and while you're at it, some lipstick wouldn't hurt."

"It's Wednesday, isn't it," she called out to me as she stood at the mirror in the ensuite. "There was a strong aroma of casseroles in the dining room."

"Yes, it's Wednesday."

Poor Judith, because Ronni is right, her dementia is becoming worse. Today's episode was proof. When she returned to the bedroom, Judith was her old self again. With my arm around her shoulders, I said, "Let's try one of those casseroles. I don't know about you, but I'm hungry."

When we arrived back in the dining room, we collected our food, thanked Daisy for keeping it warm and joined Ronni at her table. The tops of the casseroles were a little dried out but not enough to lose their flavour. For dessert, there was baked apple strudel, custard with cream and runny ice-cream.

"The police have arrived." Ronni confided in a whisper as soon as we sat down. "One of them poked her head into the dining room while you were away."

"When I asked her to hold back your casseroles, Daisy told me there were two officers, a man in plain clothes, and a lady constable."

"How did she know they were here?" I asked.

"She delivered lunch as usual to the office, and noticed Barbara talking to them in the reception area."

"Did Daisy happen to hear anything interesting? Maybe what they intended to do at the Manor?" I asked.

"She took her time," Ronni continued, "and overheard them tell Barbara the hospital had originally thought Barry took an overdose of heart medication. However, after a series of blood tests, the doctor believes there was a possibility Barry could have been poisoned."

"You mean …" I began before Judith interrupted.

"Yes," she said, her voice high and dramatic. "It's obvious the police must believe Barry was murdered."

# Chapter 10

"Don't be so melodramatic Judith," Ronni snapped. "Nobody mentioned a murder. I expect the police want to tie up any loose ends."

"Barry was murdered," Judith once again insisted. "There is no other reason for his sudden death."

"Leave it be for now," I said. "At least until we find out more from the police about what they suspect happened. In all likelihood, Barry may have overdosed on his tablets by forgetting he had already taken his pills and swallowing another lot."

"Not likely," Judith said. "because of the close attention the staff keep on our medication, it would be difficult to take a second lot."

"Maybe he found a way to get around that," Ronni remarked.

Judith pouted but said nothing as we took our dirty dishes over to the kitchen and prepared to leave the dining room.

We had almost reached the exit when, from the corner of my eye, I noticed Rita and Mrs B having a heated conversion near the kitchen door. They were nose to nose, pleading their cases, which made me wonder what their argument had been about. Mrs B seemed to be the one on top. We watched until Rita tottered backwards and disappeared into the kitchen. I may have been wrong but thought Daisy helped there with a gentle nudge to Rita's back. Mrs B turned away, pushed past us, her face red with anger, and stomped from the room. Her cane left neat marks on the linoleum as she made her way out the door and disappeared up the corridor.

Ronni gave me a prod. "I wonder what's up between her and Rita?"

"Who knows with those two," I replied as the other diners straggled out the door and turned towards their rooms. Most residents like a beauty nap after lunch but I preferred to clear my mind with a refreshing walk. "Anyway, whatever happens, the news will be out on the grapevine sooner or later."

I declined the offer of a cup of coffee in the rec room, left Ronni and Judith and returned to my apartment. In my kitchenette, I made a mug of strong, black coffee, poured in a tot of whiskey, sat on the patio, and sipped as I thought about Judith. Her state of mind had become a worry.

My memory turned back six months to another resident who had also been in the early stages of dementia. Eighty-five-year-old Evelyn Massie had been here for a week when she decided to go home. She dressed in her best suit, matching shoes, gloves, hat and handbag, ordered a taxi and somehow managed to find her way back to her old house.

The new owners had not bothered to change the locks, so Evelyn opened the front door with a spare key she had kept in her purse. It shocked the hell out of them when they arrived home after a shopping trip to find an old lady sitting on the sofa in the lounge room sipping tea and watching television. Fortunately, they remembered who she was and that she lived at the Manor, so they brought her back. We heard her indignant and loud protests as Barbara helped her along the corridor.

When she had been safely deposited back in her room, Barbara rang Evelyn's daughter who, on hearing what had happened, arranged to take Evelyn to the family doctor. After tests, they found her memory had deteriorated at a faster rate than expected, and he recommended she be placed in a nursing home.

We gave Evelyn a great send off the day she left with a double chocolate cream sponge, Rita made especially for her. But although she smiled a lot, it was apparent Evelyn did not understand what was happening.

"Oh, Judith, please try and stay sane as long as you can," I said aloud.

After finishing my coffee and whiskey, I got to my feet, stretched my back and shoulders and returned inside.

My phone had an app for my email. Now would be a good time to check for any from the publisher. Earlier this week, I had asked for an extension to the deadline for my novella. I could not concentrate on the story while not knowing whether Barry had been murdered or died from natural causes.

After discussing the novella with the publisher, I turned the phone off and sighed. Only an extension for two weeks. I hoped that would be long enough.

Now for a walk to the manager's office. Perhaps Barbara would tell me more about the police visit. She also needed to know about Judith's latest lapse. It would be better for me to let her know what happened in the dining room before she heard a garbled version through the Manor grapevine.

## Chapter 11

There was nobody at the Reception desk when I arrived. Perhaps the police were still in the office with Barbara.

A plaque on the office door read, B. Wakefield – Manager.

Faint voices could be heard from inside the room when I pressed my ear to the door. My heart thumped like a hammer as I checked to make sure the coast was still clear. Then I leaned harder to make out the words, and the door began to open.

Because my weight chose a forward movement, I stumbled into the room, tripped, fell to my knees and knocked over a soft and bulky object.

"Oomph," came from beneath me.

"Oh, bugger," came from me.

"Dimpy! What on earth …?" Barbara exclaimed as she came around from behind her desk near the window. Winded from the fall, I lay spread-eagled on the floor. She bent down with her arms out, ready to help me up, lips pursed, her eyebrows almost touching each other. It was apparent she was not impressed by my sudden appearance.

"Um, er, I'm here to discuss Judith's problem. I fear she is unwell," I said, looking up at her from my awkward position on the carpet.

It was the best I could come up with at the time. "There's

been an, er, incident in the dining room and I'm worried. I was about to knock when the door opened and caused me to lose balance and stumble through …"

Barbara wasn't listening. Instead, her eyes focused on the floor next to me. "Oh, no!" I exclaimed when I realised what had happened. In addition to landing in an undignified way, my body had fallen on top of another person. With help from Barbara, I scrambled to my feet and attempted to straighten my blouse and skirt.

Tidied to my satisfaction, I bent low and extended my hand towards the person still lying on the carpet to help them to their feet. "Oh dear, I'm so sorry," I said, and only then I realised it had been a man I had knocked over. "I hope I didn't cause you an injury," I continued, my voice filled with genuine concern.

"No, no, I'm okay, no harm done," he said as he ignored my hand, rose to his feet, bent forward and dusted himself down.

When he stood at his full height, his head only came past my shoulder. He was wearing well-tailored grey trousers, a brown jacket and a dark blue shirt and matching tie. He looked up at me with the bluest eyes I have ever seen.

There was silence while we stared at each other.

"My name is Dimpy," I said to break the silence, not sure what else to say. "I live here."

"Pleased to meet you, I'm Sergeant Plate," he replied in a formal tone.

"So, you're a policeman," I said with astonishment as he straightened his jacket and tie. "Where's your uniform? Are you tall enough? What are you, five foot eight?"

There was a strangled gasp from Barbara's direction. Too late, I realised they were not the right questions to ask. In fact, some people might think they were insensitive or 'politically incorrect' as everybody says nowadays.

With a frown, the sergeant continued to put me in my place.

"I was not on duty when called to the Manor, hence no uniform. Also, height is not a factor in the police force these days. We need to be robust and intelligent. The recruitment people are not worried about the height-weight ratio anymore. Does that explanation satisfy your problems with me?"

After the reprimand, my cheeks red with embarrassment, I nodded.

He turned towards a young, uniformed policewoman who stood next to Barbara. "My associate, Constable McKellar."

I smiled at her, and she nodded back, a big grin on her face.

My first thought was she looked too young to be a policewoman. *Stop it. It's not her fault you're old, and police officers, doctors and schoolteachers look young enough to still be in high school.*

Barbara's lips tightened as she looked at me and frowned. "This is Margaret Gruar, Sergeant Plate, known as Dimpy to her friends."

With the hope I could give the two officers the impression of normality, I smiled and tried my best to appear casual. I shook the sergeant's hand. Then I made a worse blunder of all. "Hi, pleased to meet you. I hope I didn't hurt you, Sergeant Dish."

"For goodness sake, Dimpy," Barbara said, "What is the matter with you. The sergeant's name is Plate, not … oh, never mind."

"Please accept my apologies, Sergeant Plate," I said, embarrassed even more at my clanger, "I often get muddled up nowadays."

"That's all right, er … Dimpy, isn't it?" Sergeant Plate said.

Blushing even more, I took a deep breath and changed the subject. "You're here to discuss Barry's sudden death. Do you suspect foul play? Will there be interviews? What did the coroner say?" *Shut up and stop babbling, I thought, you've made a big enough fool of yourself.*

Sergeant Plate proved to be a good sport. With a hearty laugh, he replied, "We're not sure what caused Barry Jackson's death because we do not have a report from the inquest yet. These are the early stages of our enquiries." He turned to Barbara. "I'm needed back at the station, as my normal shift is about to begin. I'll leave you in the capable hands of the constable who will check the items in question." He looked at me. "Goodbye, Dimpy. Nice to meet you." Then he nodded to each person and left the office.

Now was not the time to ask Barbara what was meant by the *items in question*. At the present moment, it was clear she was not pleased with me. We get on well, but to judge by her scowl, the information concerning Judith would have to wait.

"Perhaps it would be best if I left as well so you can continue with your work," I said to her, moving towards the door.

Then, in clipped tones, she said, "You mentioned earlier you wanted to talk about Judith's health. A more suitable time will be found for that discussion later today. Goodbye Dimpy."

I nodded farewell to her, and the constable then escaped into the corridor and shut the door behind me.

In front of the reception desk, I stopped for a moment and took a few deep breaths. My cheeks turned red as I reflected on what had happened in the office. Fancy falling over the policeman and then insulting him with garbled talk. Perhaps a walk in the park would be a chance to clear my head. I wasn't ready to tackle my secret hideout – the cleared area in the scrub – because I still had not recovered from the bandicoot episode.

# Chapter 12

After a quick return to my apartment to put on a wind jacket with a hood, I was ready for my walk.

When I opened the front door of the Manor, the cold wind gusted, and it was only by gripping the handle tightly, I managed to stop it slamming behind me. Big black clouds were streaming across the Great Western Tiers. It would soon pour with rain so it would have to be a fast walk.

I crossed over the road to the footpath which stretched along the riverbank. The river bisects the park, and there are footpaths either side where people like to walk their dogs. Sometimes, when there has been a lot of rain, the river floods across the walkways.

To the right was a shaded barbecue area with tables and chairs, popular with local people as well as tourists. Farther along, set back from the path, was a children's play area.

Dressed in warm jackets, several youngsters frolicked on swings and a slippery dip. Their voices rang out with happy laughter while their well rugged up mothers sat on a nearby seat, talking among themselves as they kept an eye on their children. A young mum rocked a pram back and forth as she chatted. Apart from myself, they were the only people in the park.

The seat I plonked onto sat between two low hedges which

gave some shelter from the wind. Today the stiff breeze made the water brown and choppy as it crept past my seat. The ducks huddled in groups along the bank. I had hoped to catch a glimpse of the platypus which frequented this part of the river, but no swirls of water showed where the animal was busy diving for food. My mind wandered to thoughts of Barry.

What were the items Sergeant Plate referred to earlier regarding Barry's medication? Had someone tampered with his tablets? But how? The drugs were kept in a locked cupboard in Barbara's office. It would be difficult for somebody, other than the staff, to tamper with the pills. There is a strict procedure to dispense them.

Each morning Barbara, or the person on duty, unlocked the cupboard and sorted the tablets into little boxes with the resident's name on each one. These were handed out before breakfast, lunch and tea as needed. A staff member always stayed close by to ensure the correct tablets went to the right person. Once used, the little cups were returned to the cupboard. Being fit for my age, I do not take prescription pills; only a magnesium supplement kept on the bench in my kitchenette.

Relax and forget Barry for a while, I said to myself.

The noise of the children playing broke into my contemplation. I stood and continued to walk, crossing the bridge to the other side of the river. Once there, I sat on a seat next to a brass statue of a platypus. Across the river, the Mountain View Manor faced towards the river.

The building was a long low structure, not what you expected from the word *Manor*. A curved drive led to the front entrance. As I watched, a taxi pulled up at the front steps. The driver got out of his seat and opened the back passenger door. Mrs B emerged from the cab, on her way home from goodness knows where. She shrugged off the driver's hand when he attempted to assist her by holding her arm. Instead, she used her stick to stand upright, said something to the driver and stomped towards the entrance, the wind whipping up the edges of her coat as she walked.

The taxi driver must have found something on the back seat because he called out to her. When she stopped and turned around, he walked over and handed her a small parcel.

There was no apology or thanks; she snatched the package, continued up the steps and disappeared into the Manor. The taxi driver shrugged, banged the back-seat door shut, got in the driver's seat and spun the wheels as he left.

In the Manor, there are four large apartments with patios along the back of the building. I have one, next to me is Carol, then Barry's empty room and Judith has number four. The rec room comes next, then the dining room and kitchen. Seven smaller units extend along both sides of a corridor at the left of the reception area, fourteen in all. The same number of units continue either side of another passage on the right-hand side. Including the patio rooms, there are four apartments and twenty-eight private units. Apart from the patio apartments, each one contains a bed-sitting room with ensuite and a tiny kitchenette, with two overhead cupboards, a microwave oven, sink, electric jug and small bench.

As you walk into the main entrance, Barbara's office is next to the reception desk, and her living quarters and a staffroom are opposite our patio apartments. Behind the kitchen is a laundry for residents and staff use. Four washing machines and two dryers sit at one wall, storage cupboards for blankets, sheets and pillows and ironing board on another. A sliding glass door leads out to an enclosed drying area, with folding clotheslines attached to a wall.

In the park, the wind picked up, and drops of rain fell onto my hands and head. No sounds came from the playground. The mothers and their children had left while I sat in contemplation. Just as well, I thought. The black clouds now hung overhead; there would be a downpour soon. With my jacket zipped up, I hurried back through the park and across the road to the Manor.

There was one thought in my mind as I opened the front door. What on earth could be wrong with Barry's tablets that would cause the police to become involved in his sudden death?

## Chapter 13

After he returned to the police station after he visited the Mountain View Residential Manor, Sergeant Plate sat at his desk and leaned back in the chair. He placed both arms across his chest and sighed.

Two days ago, the sergeant usually in charge at the Kinross Police Station had caught a plane to Sydney, where he would attend a course about drug smuggling. After that, he intended to take three months long service leave on the Gold Coast in Queensland with his wife and two teenage children.

Although based in Launceston, Plate had been called to the Tasmanian Police Headquarters in Hobart and told to take charge of the police station in Kinross until the return of the regular sergeant

Anticipating a trouble-free transfer, the Manor problem could not have happened at the worst time. With three court cases to prepare for trial in the next six weeks, it meant finding time to write up notes for each one. Meanwhile, files and folders awaiting his attention lay stacked in a messy heap next to the computer. He had packed everything into a cardboard box and brought the lot to Kinross to continue working on them. Any information he needed would be buried somewhere in the pile of files on his desk or hidden deep in the box.

His thoughts turned to the death at the Mountain View Residential Manor. The pathologist wanted Barry Jackson's current medication checked. Specifically, the dosage and how it was administered. The hospital staff suspected foul play, but at the moment, there was no proof. There was nothing more to done until the inquest report became available in a couple of days.

His tummy gave a rumble, which reminded him that due to the time spent at the Manor, he had missed his lunch break. He opened the bottom drawer, removed a brown paper bag and placed it on his desk. From the bag, he withdrew a bacon and egg sandwich bought earlier from a local shop on his way to the Manor. While taking a bite of the sandwich, his memory drifted to the woman who had fallen into the manager's office and tripped over him.

The need to discuss someone called Judith with the manager had been a decoy; his years of policing told him that. She was far too twitchy. A nosey old biddy, he thought, lots of them around and they all assume they knew more than the police.

He placed his half-eaten sandwich on the desk, pushed the chair back and strolled over to the coffee machine in the right-hand corner of the office. Coffee making facilities were one of the perks of the job. He made a strong mug of black coffee, ignored the sugar and small jug of milk and took it back to his desk, picked up his sandwich and took a bite. While drinking the coffee, he looked around the room and noticed the other two untidy desks were empty.

A large window in the office had a view that looked out to the front of the police station. In the reception area, a male constable stood behind a counter. He was talking to a tearful young woman holding the hand of a little boy. The lad had a rebellious look as he glared at the policeman. He wondered if he should intervene then decided the officer would call him if he needed help.

Instead, his attention turned to watching Constable McKellar climb from the passenger side of a police vehicle. The officer driving the car waited until she exited and then pulled back onto the road and sped off. The wind had intensified, and rain fell in big drops as she ran across the car park to the police station. One hand held a briefcase, the other lay on top of her head, holding down her hat to keep off the rain.

After a few minutes, a dripping wet Constable McKellar came into the room through the back entrance. She took off the hat, shook it free of raindrops and draped it across a rack next to the door.

"It's raining," she said as she removed her rain jacket and placed it onto a hook next to the hat.

"Yes, I can see that." Sergeant Plate replied, "I noticed dark clouds were gathering over the Tiers while I drove back here from the Manor."

Before she had time to sit in the seat opposite him, he added, "What happened after I left?"

Constable McKellar took a notebook from her shirt pocket and checked her notes. She leaned over the desk and outlined everything she had done during the afternoon.

"As we'd arranged in advance, I stayed behind to have a good look around and familiarise myself with the place," she said. "As requested, I checked the drugs register with Barbara Wakefield, the lady we met this morning."

The sergeant drank his coffee, placed the mug on the desk and said, "Was everything in order?"

"It all seemed in order. Barbara Wakefield assured me they always observed the correct protocol when giving out medication." She stopped talking and sat on a chair in front of the desk. "I also checked this information with the staff on duty yesterday. They swore there were no changes to their routine and were positive the drugs were dispensed as prescribed."

"What about the night staff?"

Constable McKellar turned over the page in her notebook and scanned what she had written. "Apart from Barbara Wakefield, who lives on the premises, there is a nurse who comes in to work the night-shift from 10 pm to 6 am. Two temps from an agency work two shifts on Sundays to give Barbara and Andrea a break." She licked her finger and turned to the next page on her pad. "After a phone call from Barbara, the night nurse came to the Manor straight away. Her name is Andrea Green, who will doubtless give me a cold; she had a beauty herself; sneezed the whole time we spoke."

"You'll survive; a little cold won't stop you from doing your job. Anything else of interest to report?"

"Because of her cold, Andrea Green was off duty on the night in question. Barbara Wakefield took her shift."

"Did you still ask her about her usual duties as a night nurse?"

"The routine questions were the same ones put to Barbara Wakefield. Andrea Green was adamant the night-time medication was always dispensed in the correct way when she is on duty."

"And the temps for last Sunday?"

"Barbara Wakefield rang the agency, and I spoke to Judith Anderson, and Gloria Bakes, who were the temporary nurses on duty that day and night. Both Miss Anderson and Mrs Bakes assured me over the phone that under their supervision, the correct medication was always given out."

Sergeant Plate sipped his coffee, then put the mug back on the desk. "Good job, Maureen. From your report, there doesn't seem to be any reason to accuse anyone on the staff of misconduct or carelessness. In fact, they seem to run a tight ship at the Manor."

Constable McKellar found a tissue in her pocket, blew her nose and squirmed. She felt uncomfortable when her boss reverted to calling her by her Christian name. It always confused her. Was she supposed to call her boss, James? Informality made her uncomfortable.

For this reason, the decision was easy. To act as she would to any superior officer. "Thank you, sergeant."

"Let's consider it a job well done and send a report of your findings to the pathologist and coroner. Tell them we have finished the investigation and are satisfied with the handling of Barry Jackson's medication." He gave a sudden grin. "I don't think anybody murdered the poor old guy. At least not deliberately."

"It's still an unusual case, sir." Constable McKellar said. "Mr Jackson dying in such a strange way."

"We had a case similar to this a few years ago when I was a constable in Hobart." He stopped talking, finished his drink and placed the empty mug on the desk. "Turned out the chap had been to four different doctors and given similar prescriptions by each one. He was taking all the prescribed tablets every day. This caused the bloke's veins to become too thin to hold blood, so they burst. The ambulance rushed him to the hospital, but there was nothing anyone could do to save him."

To change the subject, he said, "Grab a coffee and although it's late, eat your lunch, while I ring the hospital. I'll advise them of our findings regarding the medication and tell them a written report is on the way."

A cup of tea would be preferable, she thought. Once the tea was made and being careful not to spill it, she walked over to her desk and sat down. She placed the cup on the desktop and opened the bottom drawer. With one hand she took out a lunch box and set it on the desk. Clicking the latch open, she removed a salad roll, unwrapped it and began to eat.

Sergeant Plate hung up the phone and turned to her. "The pathologist said he is happy with the report. When we receive the results of the autopsy from the hospital, he wants a written copy as soon as possible. He needs to put it with the details from the inquest." He thought for a moment while finishing his sandwich. "Make a duplicate report as well for the coroner. Once we send both statements on our findings to the relevant authorities, we can close the case concerning Barry Jackson's death."

As he placed the plastic from the sandwich wrap into a rubbish bin, he continued talking. "Now, constable, what is your opinion of our gate crasher, Dimpy?"

Constable McKellar swallowed a mouthful of her roll before replying. "She's a real character. Nice looking for an old girl. Did you see her dimples?"

He ignored the question and commented: "She was an odd one, though. Somewhat flighty, I'd say, but one with a plan which did not involve a drop in for a chat about someone called Judith."

Sergeant Plate stroked his chin, deep in thought. "I wonder what she wanted. I don't suppose you caught sight of her again, did you?"

"No, sir, I didn't."

"Very well, let's leave it at that. Perhaps our Dimpy was plain nosey." He became more business-like. "When you've finished your lunch, type up your notes about the medication and leave it on my desk before you leave for home this afternoon. Nothing more can be done until all results of the investigation are added to the file."

He started to put the documents on his desk in order and handed over a folder marked 'Jackson, Barry' to the constable. "Once all the information is collated, we can stamp the file as a closed case. I believe we have more than enough to get on with at the moment," he added, turning to the files cluttering up the top of his desk.

# Chapter 14

On Friday, three days after Barrie's death, I woke early from a good night's sleep – no dead bodies and no Carol falling out of bed. I glanced at my watch. It was 7.15 am. The doona pushed aside, I arose, dressed and made my way to breakfast at an earlier time than usual. However, for no reason I could think of, Mrs B still glared at me as she ticked my name.

At the buffet table, Rita was filling the dishes on the warming platters with bacon, tomatoes, scrambled and fried eggs. I picked up a tray and scanned the room. The dining room was half full, but Ronni, Don and Judith were not among those present. Not wanting a hot breakfast, I made my selection of a packet of cereal, small jug of milk, two slices of toast, butter and apricot jam. I added a cup of tea, and with both hands holding the tray, I made my way to a table near the kitchen. Once seated, I poured the milk over my cereal and began to eat.

As I buttered my toast, Ronni and Don arrived, and their voices could be heard from where they stood at the buffet table chatting to each other while deciding on their choices for breakfast. No sign of Judith which, because of the event yesterday at lunch when she turned up in her nightie, caused me some disquiet.

"It's okay, Dimpy ol' girl," Don said as he placed his tray on the table. "Don't look so friggin' worried. Judith's daughter picked her up early this morning."

"That's right," Ronni said as she joined us. "They passed me in the corridor on their way out. After breakfast in a local café, they're going to an auction. I've told Mrs B, and she put a big tick next to Judith's name."

"She's always at friggin' auctions," Dan chimed in.

"Judith loves going to auctions with her family," Ronni said, glaring at Don. "Her daughter's husband used to be an antique dealer before he retired and what's wrong with him still liking to attend auctions?"

"Okay, keep your friggin' hat on. I was only sayin' …" He gave up and shook salt and pepper over his scrambled eggs.

Judith has a considerate daughter, Dianne, who lives in town with her retired husband, Graeme Mackintosh, who is a collector of antique Toby jugs. When they go to auctions, they always take Judith with them for the day. Judith and her daughter go shopping while Graeme bids on the jugs.

Dianne has two grown-up sons who both live and work at the mines in Western Australia. Judith's happiest days are when they come back to Tasmania to visit, and they can have a newsy time together.

Almost ready to thank them for the explanation about Judith's whereabouts, I noticed Barbara standing at the door. She craned her neck, looked around the room, then walked past Mrs B without acknowledging her and made a beeline towards our table. I wondered what she wanted as Barbara always ate meals alone in her office. Manager's privilege, I suppose. She nodded and smiled at residents as she walked past their tables.

On arrival, she bent over and in a low voice said, "Dimpy, would you mind following me to my office? I would like a word with you in private."

What was so urgent Barbara should disturb my breakfast? I murmured apologetic goodbyes to my friends, left my half-eaten toast on the table, and followed her from the room.

## Chapter 15

"Sit down Dimpy," she said once we reached the office. "Sorry to drag you away from breakfast and your friends, but there is a lot to do today." She sat behind the desk and continued speaking. "Because of your impromptu appearance in my office yesterday it was obvious Barry's sudden death worried you more than Judith's erratic behaviour."

"Yes, it did," I replied and sat back in the chair, ready to listen.

"Barry's death was most traumatic," Barbara said. "However, Constable McKellar had rung his doctor for a list of all his medications. She brought the list with her and did a thorough check with the staff about all Barry's pills, including his heart tablets."

Barbara stopped talking and took a deep breath. "Sergeant Plate was kind enough to ring early this morning with the coroner's decision from the inquest yesterday. He was satisfied the right procedure was followed by everyone who dealt with Barry's daily tablets. This included information leading up to and during the week that Barry passed away."

"Oh, okay," I said.

"Nevertheless, the reason the pathologist at the hospital had a few concerns about Barry's death was because the post-mortem found a large quantity of digitalis in his body." Before I could say anything, she continued talking. "After the police report had been received, the coroner concluded that Barry might have taken other medication in addition to those he took here." Barbara stopped talking and looked at me. "Is all this making sense to you Dimpy?"

"Yes," I replied.

"After taking into account all the information in the report Sergeant Plate presented to the court, the coroner decided Barry's demise would be recorded as 'death by misadventure'. Because of this, the police have called off the investigation, and the case is closed."

Barbara stood and plucked a piece of paper from the desk. "After a complete check, I found there was no close relative listed in his file as I had originally thought. Because of this, I decided to make the funeral arrangements myself."

She walked around her desk, handed the paper to me then returned to her seat and continued to speak as I read it. "I intend contacting his solicitor this morning to confirm that we can go ahead with a funeral as stated in his will. Fortunately, there was a copy in his file. After I have the go-ahead from the solicitor, this announcement will be pinned on the notice board this afternoon." She nodded towards the paper in my hand. "The service is to be conducted at the Kinross funeral home at 11.00 next Monday morning followed by a private cremation."

I passed the paper back to her as she continued to speak. "Although taxis can be ordered for anyone who needs them, I think most people will be happy to walk to the funeral home from here. It is only a short distance from the Manor."

She glanced at my face. "Is everything okay?" she said when I did not reply straight away. "You still appear concerned. Your dimples are twitching."

"Barry's death caused by an overdose of digitalis?" I shook

my head. "No, Barbara, I find that decision difficult to believe. Barry always complained about the number of pills he *had* to take. I am certain he would never have taken extra medicine on the sly."

I stood up, ready to leave. "Thank you for organising Barry's funeral, and I appreciate you taking the trouble to let me know the result of the investigation. It has given me a lot to think about."

Barbara gave me a puzzled glance as I left the room.

# Chapter 16

Not many people attended the funeral; only me, Judith, Ronni, Barbara and four of his personal friends from the Manor. The one individual who always loved funerals was not there. Mrs B had a bad cold and decided she was too ill to come with us.

Although the weather was overcast, we decided to walk as a group to the funeral home. Barbara had already told us Barry's will stated he preferred not to have a ceremony at the church.

We filed into the chapel at the funeral parlour and eyed some strangers standing at the entrance to the room. The man approached Barbara and introduced himself as a relative of Barry's. He was a nephew from Barry's wife's' side of the family, whom nobody at the Manor knew existed. Apart from himself, his wife and two teenage children, twelve people sat in the front two rows.

I was glad we were there. Barry had often made me laugh with his outrageous and sometimes crude sense of humour.

He had moved into the Manor when his wife died five years earlier. They had both been solicitors and did not have any children of their own. Barry had told me they married in their late fifties; a first marriage, as neither had been married before. They were introduced at a combined lunch put on by their respective firms, and according to Barry, it had been love at first sight.

The funeral was a brief ceremony. After a few sober words from the funeral director, and the hymn, Amazing Grace, was sung, Barbara stood and invited everyone to return to the Manor for refreshments. Six men from the funeral home walked the coffin out through a side exit to the crematorium. We filed out the front door into the cold day with a touch of the sun that showed now and then through the cloud cover.

As we walked back to the Manor, Barbara told me Barry's will stated his savings were to be used to pay for the funeral and reception. It contained no mention of any inheritance for the nephew who had turned up out of the blue.

"After the service, his nephew told me he only found out Barry was dead when he saw the obituary notice in the newspaper. However, the family wanted to attend and show their respects."

Two long trestle tables had been erected in the dining room. Rita and Daisy had been kept busy since breakfast with the food preparation. Plates of finger food, party pies, sausage rolls, sandwiches and chocolate sponge cake were on offer. Glasses held red and white wine and orange juice. An urn bubbled away for those who preferred tea or coffee. I mingled for a while among the mourners, lending a sympathetic ear as they talked about their memories of Barry.

His nephew told me he intended to scatter the ashes at Lobster Point where, in his younger days, Barry often went fishing.

While I helped myself to sandwiches and a piece of chocolate cake, Ronni chatted to Barry's nephew and his wife. His children sat on chairs facing the picture window with iPods glued to their ears. After a few bites of the sandwich, my eyes darted around the room looking for Judith, but couldn't spot her anywhere. Perhaps she had gone back to her apartment; it might be worth a check. After swallowing a last piece of cake, and drinking my tea, I returned my empty plate, cup and saucer to the kitchen.

Without being noticed, I left the gathering and wandered along the corridor to Judith's apartment.

My hand froze in the air as I lifted it to knock on her door. Muffled voices sounded from inside., Judith's and a deep male rumble, which was rising in volume. It must be her son Todd; I'd met him once before. He only turned up to hassle her for money.

When I knocked, the voices stopped before Judith called out, "Who's there?"

"It's Dimpy. I decided to come and have a drink with you to toast Barry." I said.

When the door opened a harassed looking Judith gave me a shaky smile and said, "Come in."

"No, she can't come in. Get rid of the old bag; we're busy," her son called out in an angry voice

The rough tone halted me in my tracks, but Judith surprised me. Turning to face him, she said, "This is my home, Todd, and I'll invite anyone I want into it." She waved me through the open door. "Sorry about that, Dimpy," she said, giving me a brief hug. "Todd gets carried away sometimes." She looked towards her son. "He's about to leave."

Todd's looks and behaviour had changed little since the last time I'd seen him a few months ago. The same shabby, unkempt appearance – uncombed, greasy hair, shirt hanging over a beer belly. A dirty, grey tee shirt had the words "It's a shitty world" across the front. Judith had told me Todd was fifty-three. He had the veiny red face of a heavy drinker and an attitude to match. Pursed lips gave him the look of a petulant child who didn't like the fact they were not getting their way.

He glared at both of us, strode to the still-open door, turned and said, "Don't forget what I told you. I'll come back another time when you're alone. We'll finish our conversation then." With a slam of the door he left.

After a moment, Judith turned towards me with a drawn, sad expression on her face. "Oh, Dimpy, I'm so glad you came because I don't know what to do. Todd wants me to sell my house and give the money to him and Dianne. I've no real use for the house anymore he says and argues the money would be of more help to him." Tears welled up in her eyes.

"What does Dianne say about the treatment you're receiving from Todd?"

Judith shook her head. "Nothing. From what she lets slip on her visits, I am sure my son tells lies, saying I don't need the home anymore and want to sell it."

"A young couple has leased it, haven't they?"

"That's right. The rental agent said the house and garden are immaculate and above all the rent they pay comes in handy for extra expenses. As you know, Dimpy, the pension is not a lot to live on by itself."

Tears formed in her eyes as Judith grew more and more distraught. Time to change the subject. I pointed to the kettle next to a powerpoint on a bench in the kitchenette. "Let's not talk about what your son has been up to until some other time. Right now, it would be much nicer to toast Barry with a cup of tea and forget ungrateful children for a while."

Judith gave a weak smile and nodded agreement, then walked across to a cabinet to fetch cups and saucers. I breathed a sigh of relief; she'd be happier after a hot drink and gossip.

After visiting Judith, I decided not to return to the wake. A cigarette began to call my name. As it was late afternoon and becoming cold and gloomy, I put on a windcheater and twirled a scarf around my neck.

The weather had become windy and tossed the ends of my scarf every which way as I crossed the patio and headed for my hideaway in the clearing.

Before sitting on the log, I gave a glance around the area for any movement. The bandicoot must be in the hollow, I assumed, as I listened for any scratching noises. Satisfied all was quiet, I sat down, reached for my cigarettes and lit up.

A few puffs later, scuffling noises came from inside the log. After several minutes, the bandicoot scampered out and disappeared into the bush, followed by two youngsters who, by their size and scarcity of fur, had not long been born. Obviously, my companion was not a male.

Shadows crept into the clearing. I shivered. The weather had become too chilly to stay outside any longer.

One last puff before I stubbed the cigarette out, and returned the packet, lighter and ashtray into the log. With the hope I wouldn't have disturbed the bandicoot family into moving to another home, I hurried back to the warmth of my room.

The sandwiches and cake at Barry's wake had filled me up, so I decided not to worry about going to the dining room for tea. I thought about finding Ronni to discuss Todd's visit with his mother but chose not to bother. Instead, I would keep a close eye on Judith, and perhaps with a bit of thought, might discover a way to stop Todd upsetting her.

I showered and changed into my nightie and dressing gown. Then swivelled the television to face my recliner and watched old movies until I felt tired enough to go to sleep.

## Chapter 17

Two days after Barry's funeral, Carol fell out of bed again, and this time she landed on the floor with an extra heavy thump. Her screams of agony were so loud I sprang out of bed and dressed only in my nightie rushed into her room. I found her lying on the carpet, and it was apparent she was in a lot of pain. An ambulance took her to the local hospital where they discovered under the rolls of fat; she had dislocated her shoulder.

Next morning after breakfast, I rang the hospital to check how she was getting on. They paged a nurse who told me Mrs Wilson's shoulder had been replaced in the socket. However, because of her size, she would need to stay in the hospital another day for observation. The nurse explained it was a precaution to make sure the arm remained in the correct position before they would allow her to be discharged.

Early the next day, I once again rang the hospital to be told Mrs Wilson could go home after lunch that afternoon. I ordered a taxi for one o'clock. When we reached the hospital, the driver waited while I collected Carol from the reception area. Her arm was in a sling, and it was noticeable the ordeal had left her tired and worn out.

"When the doctor managed to put the shoulder back in position the relief from the terrible pain was wonderful," she said as the driver held open the front passenger door for her. "It's still painful when I move my arm. The hospital arranged an appointment with my doctor for tomorrow morning at 10.00 o'clock. Just to check my health and arm are still okay."

"I am going to buy another bed, Dimpy. This fall made me realise I have put it off for far too long. Will you please come with me?"

As we walked to her room, we arranged to visit Launceston to buy a new bed the next day after her doctor's appointment at the Kinross Medical Clinic.

What an ordeal that became, and, for me, total embarrassment.

The weather for bed buying day began cold and clear. The Great Western Tiers were free of rainclouds. During breakfast, I asked my friends if they wanted to come into Launceston with us while Carol bought her bed.

"I'd come with you," Don said, "but the thought of friggin' Carol tryin' out beds in full view of everyone in the store could put me off my friggin' lunch."

Judith declined as she had arranged to go shopping with her daughter. Ronni agreed to join us and keep me company while Carol checked out beds. After breakfast, we walked back to our rooms to tidy up and change into suitable clothes for a trip to the city. In my case, that meant a lilac pants suit, black skivvy and sensible walking shoes. Carol also wore a pants suit, dark blue in size extra, extra-large.

Ronni, in a beautiful cut jacket and skirt in swirling pink and lime green and a pink blouse, joined us as the taxi Carol hired to take us to the doctor's clinic, pulled up in front of the Manor door. Carol sat in the front seat and Don fit himself into the back with Ronni and me. He had changed his mind at the last minute and decided to accompany us as far as the shopping centre.

"I'll wait in the pub, have a beer and a yarn with the regulars.

It'll give me something friggin' to do. Give me a ring when you're ready to leave for home."

At the clinic, we waited in the reception area for the doctor to give Carol the all-clear and remove the sling. We hopped on a bus outside the clinic and headed for the Launceston to visit furniture shops that specialised in beds.

We parted ways with Don at the bus depot in Launceston, walked to the next street and entered our first furniture store.

That's where the fun began.

From then on, Carol insisted on trying all the double beds on display in every store we visited. With complaints about her arm hurting, guess who heaved her up each time she lay down. Me, that's who. Sometimes Ronni had to push while I pulled. Thank goodness Carol had worn a pants suit. My mind visualised what she would have looked like wearing a dress and shuddered. The salespeople tried to keep straight faces, which must have been difficult as they watched an extra-large lady bounce on their beds.

At the third shop, Ronni took off by herself. "I can't stand it anymore. Everyone is watching us and laughing hysterically. When Carol's decided on a bed, ring me on your mobile, and I'll meet you back at the bus stop."

After helping Carol off a bed for the umpteenth time, I lost patience. My back ached from the strain of hauling her plump body upright from a prone position. It was time for a decision, I told her in my best imitation of a sergeant major.

"I am going to wait outside on the pavement while you choose one of these beds, pay, and arrange for delivery to the Manor."

"All okay Dimpy, I've bounced and turned on this bed, and it felt wonderful. I don't think I'll ever fall out. I'll buy some extra-large sheets and a new doona, and we'll be ready to leave."

The shell-shocked sales assistant gave an audible sigh of relief when told Carol would take the bed.

I stood on the pavement outside the shop, took a deep breath to calm down and prayed for a cigarette. Not that it would not have helped because I never smoked in the street and it may be illegal nowadays.

As I gazed around at the passing parade of people, I spotted a familiar figure walking into a chemist shop on the other side of the road—Emily Barraclough's son. For no particular reason, I decided to see what he was doing there.

Once inside the shop, I spied him standing near the back wall behind the prescription counter, putting on a white coat. Was he a chemist? If so, surely Mrs B would have bragged to everyone over and over again about her wonderful sons' occupation.

I pointed him out to the lady standing behind the perfume counter. "Is the man in the white coat the chemist?"

"No," she said, "Mr Barraclough is an assistant. His job is to check the prescriptions before handing them to the chemist to be made up. He also ensures the customers receive the correct medications before coming to the till to pay. People often have questions about new medicines. Answering them is also part of his job."

"Mr Barraclough is kept busy then."

"Oh, yes," she replied.

Before he spotted me, I left the store and crossed the road to where Carol was standing, gazing around with a worried look. Her face cleared when I walked towards her.

"There you are, Dimpy," she said. "We can leave now; the store will deliver my new bed and sheets this afternoon at about four o'clock. As soon as we get back home, I must tell the groundsmen so they can erect the bed when it arrives. I checked the timetable kept in my purse, and a bus to Kinross will be here in fifteen minutes."

I made a quick phone call to Ronni and Don, and they arrived at the bus depot with five minutes to spare before the bus was due to leave.

"Made it by the skin of our friggin' teeth, eh Dimpy," Don said as he and Ronni walked along the aisle to where Carol and I sat on the back seat. Plenty of room there for Carol to spread out. "Where's your new bed, Carol?"

"Don't be silly, Don, I don't have it with me," Carol replied. "The store has agreed to take my old bed away when they deliver my new one. They looked dubious at first, but I insisted they do this, or I'd look elsewhere."

I shuddered. Another round of beds? No way.

We arrived home just in time for lunch. Afterwards, I joined an excited Carol in the rec room for coffee before returning to my apartment for a well-earned rest.

The delivery van with Carol's bed arrived at ten past three. While Carol supervised the installation, Ronni and I sat in the rec room and enjoyed a cup of tea. Don's few hours in the hotel had caused him to feel a little under the weather. Straight after lunch, he disappeared into his room for a nap.

The groundsmen had already put the old bed in a storage shed, a short distance behind the main building, ready to be picked up by the delivery men and taken back to Launceston.

After the van left, Ronni and I strolled to Carol's room, with a few of the residents and watched from the doorway as Carol tucked in the new sheets and plumped the pillowcases. Then she put the finishing touch of the new doona on top.

As this bed was more extensive than the previous one, her bedside table had to be moved, which meant less room for her two large recliners. Carol directed Ronni and me to change their positions around a few times until she was satisfied and thanked us for our help. Then I went back to my room, collapsed on my bed and had an exhausting snooze.

I vowed never to go bed shopping with Carol again.

# Chapter 18

There was speculation throughout the Manor about who would be the lucky person to move into Barry's vacant apartment. There was no contest though, because most residents realised Don was next in line. He had been a resident for almost as long as Carol, Judith, and me.

After informing Don of the Board of Managements foregone decision, Barbara put the announcement on the notice board to say that Don Ahegge would transfer into Barry's apartment on the following Monday.

Don's mates from the bowling club helped move his furniture and boxes from his former unit next to Mrs B's. She stood in the doorway of the patio apartment and glared at them. They ignored her and continued to unpack as she stomped away in disgust, making as much racket as she could with the cane.

"Glad to get away from the old bitch, Dimpy," he told me later. "Kept waylaying me with friggin' grizzles and spite about people in the Manor. Friggin' nasty she was when told I was moving into a patio room. I thought she would hit me with her friggin' cane."

I'd decided my apartment was long overdue for a housework morning. Time to change the sheets, doona cover and pillow slips. They, plus towels and tea towels lay in a heap before being picked up, carted to the laundry and put in the washing machine.

While waiting for the machine to finishing washing, I remade the bed with fresh linen, hung clean towels in the ensuite, and placed new tea towels into a rack inside the kitchen cupboard. As I still felt motivated, the floors received an energetic mop, and the door to the shower recess shone after a wipe down with glass cleaner.

After dusting the furniture and vacuuming the carpet, I went back to the laundry and pulled the washing out the machine. As it looked like being a sunny day with a slight breeze, I hung everything on a clothesline outside the laundry to dry.

Back in my room, I showered, changed out of the tracksuit I had been wearing to do my chores and donned a cheerful red and green tartan skirt and a sky-blue mohair twinset, with a pair of flat lace-up shoes. After a quick brush of my hair and a touch of makeup using the now spotless bathroom mirror, there was still time before lunch for a ten-minute walk to the bottle shop.

As I entered the store, I was surprised to see the assistant at the counter, putting a few cans of beer in a paper bag for Mrs B.

"Hello Emily, I didn't know you drank beer." The astonishment was evident in my voice.

"Of course, I don't drink alcohol, Dimpy. These are for my son." She grabbed the bag from the counter and hugged them to her chest as she left the shop.

With my purchase paid for, I hurried back to the Manor, placed the whiskey bottle in the kitchen cupboard and made my way to the dining room for a fish and chip lunch. As I stood at the luncheon buffet deciding whether to have crumbed whiting or battered flake with my chips and salad, there came a sense of somebody standing alongside. No one stood there at head height, so my eyes dropped to waist level and saw someone holding a large container of chips in both hands.

"Excuse me," she said, "These chips need to be popped into a warming tray."

I took one step back and spotted the edges of a curly blonde head poking out from under a white cap. "Who are …" I started to ask.

Daisy, bringing another tray of cooked fish from the kitchen, arrived in time to help me out. "This is my new off-sider, Molly. Rita is no longer employed at the Manor, so Molly's stepped in to take her place. She might be small but is a real whirlwind in the kitchen."

"Hi Molly, nice to meet you. Please call me Dimpy".

Molly put the chips on the buffet table and reached up to shake hands. "My, you are tall, aren't you?" she said as if her size was the norm.

Taken aback by her bluntness, it took a moment or two for me to react. "Yes, people sometimes make comments about my height." Then, not content to leave it there, I continued, "But I should warn you about my big feet. You must be careful I don't trip over you. I'm inclined to fall on people. Even normal-size ones let alone little folk." Molly blinked, then gave my feet a thoughtful look.

"Anyway," I continued, trying to recover my dignity. "Welcome to the Manor."

"Thank you," she giggled and trotted back to the kitchen with the empty chips tray. A few minutes later, I saw her racing from one empty table to another stacking and removing the dirty dishes. Daisy was right; Molly was a miniature whirlwind.

Daisy poked her head out of the kitchen door and beckoned to me. "I thought you should know why Molly is here. The management has sacked Rita."

"Goodness me," I said. "Whatever happened? She always seemed a good worker if a trifle surly sometimes."

Hands on hips, Daisy replied, "Mrs B happened, that's who. They had a huge argument the day before yesterday; in fact, it looked as if they would tear each other's hair out." With a frown, she shook her head. "Like chalk and cheese the both of them."

"Judith, Ronni and I saw them quarrelling in the dining room a few weeks ago. They always seemed to be bickering at each other. What was this disagreement over?"

"Mrs B was forever complaining about the quality of the food. As you are aware, Dimpy, we always try to give everybody the best the Manor can afford, and no one else has ever complained."

"So, what did Mrs B say was wrong with the food?"

"The old bitch wanted expensive meals such as crayfish, fillet steak, scallops and fancy desserts. She asked the management to hire a proper chef, which is out of the question. Imagine the expense. Chef's do not come cheap." Daisy heaved a big sigh. "Rita tried to explain the cost of high-priced food was too expensive for our budget, but Mrs B would not believe her".

Daisy looked back into the kitchen to make sure everything was in order. "Rita lost her temper and told Mrs B where she could put her expensive food, so Mrs B stomped to Barbara's office and complained. Still not satisfied, she wrote to the Board claiming Rita had been rude to her."

Molly came tearing past us into the kitchen, grabbed a plate of fish and chips then raced out the door towards Barbara's office.

Daisy waited until she passed by before continuing. "When the Board backed Mrs B because a staff member had been rude to a resident, Barbara had no option but to dismiss her. Rita's temper often got her into trouble, and this was the last straw."

"I'm sorry to hear the news about Rita losing her job. She was a good worker, and I liked the food she cooked. Plain but tasty. However, with her experience, she should have no trouble finding another position."

Daisy nodded. "Barbara, without the Board knowing, gave Rita a good reference. Although not exactly friends, they often chatted together over coffee when planning the menus."

"And is the Board going to hire a chef?"

Daisy let out a gale of laughter. "No, of course not. Barbara told me they informed Mrs B if she wanted expensive dinners, she would have to supply the gourmet food."

We watched Molly race back through the dining room into the kitchen.

I turned back to Daisy. "I guess she will have to stand on your shoulders to reach the overhead cupboards."

"Yes, but the upside is no sore back reaching into the bottom ones. I do hope Molly will stay; she has such a bubbly personality."

With a small sigh, Daisy returned to the kitchen while I continued to prepare my lunch. Battered flake, chips with a lettuce, tomato and cheese salad. To be followed by lemon sponge pudding and cream. No complaints from me about the food at the Manor.

Unfortunately, Don's stay in a patio room did not last long. A week after he moved into his patio apartment, Don became ill. On a Friday lunchtime to be exact, fish and chips day.

# Chapter 19

On Friday morning, I had a guilty thought that my novella could do with some work. With no disturbances, perhaps I could finish the first draft by lunchtime. Satisfied by late morning with what had been completed, I turned off the computer and made my way to the dining-room.

Don, Ronni and Judith were sitting at a table close to the window well away from the kitchen area. Always a little worried I would be knocked over by the whirling dervish called Molly, I edged towards them. On reaching the table, I saw Ronni and Judith frowning as they stared at Don.

"What's the matter? Is something wrong with Don?"

"Yes," Judith said. "A few minutes ago he appeared okay, now he looks terrible. He's gone as white as a ghost."

I placed the tray on the table and also stared at him. His forehead looked clammy. Droplets of sweat clung to his brows. I put my finger on the pulse in his neck. The rate was much too fast.

"Where do you feel sick, Don? In the tummy, or …?"

"Not so friggin' good all over, Dimpy. Any moment now I'm gonna friggin' spew. Perhaps I might be better lying on the bed in my room for a bit."

"Good idea, Don. You do so while we explain to Barbara,

you're unwell. She will come to your apartment later and check you out." I turned to Ronni and Judith. "Look at him, it's obvious he's running a temperature, and his pulse is racing. I have never seen him so ill before. I'll let Barbara know while one of you helps him to his room."

Don overheard me. "Don't need any help goin' to my friggin' room; I'll manage." Then he added, "Thanks all the same." As he was not always a reasonable man, there seemed no point trying to argue with him. He staggered as he pulled himself from the chair, stood and swayed for a moment before he shuffled from the dining room into the corridor.

As soon as possible, Barbara would have to be told that Don was not well. Leaving Ronni and Judith to finish their meal, I took my lunch back to the kitchen and explained about Don feeling sick. Daisy agreed to keep my meal warm until I returned from talking to Barbara. Then I headed for her office.

Barbara's lips tightened as she shook her head. "Don? Ill? Most unusual; even at eighty-two, he's the healthiest man I've ever seen for his age. He never gets sick, at least, not until now anyway." She picked up the phone, rang the doctor and asked him to call in to see Don later in the afternoon. After the call, she turned to me and said, "I still can't believe he is unwell. The man has the constitution of an ox. What were his symptoms?"

I told what I'd observed. This was decision time. "I'm going to Don's room to check on him," I said.

"Good idea. I'll come as well," she replied, pushing her unfinished lunch to one side.

In the corridor, a fleeting glance took in Mrs B going past us in the opposite direction, heading towards the rec room. Being a busy body, I wondered if she would stop us and demand to be told why we were in such a hurry. However, this time she ignored us, and we hurried on our way to Don's apartment.

"From what you told me about Don's symptoms, I will be

pleased when I can see for myself how ill he has become," Barbara said as we continued at a fast pace down the corridor.

When we arrived, I knocked on Don's door. There was no answer, so I called out. "Are you there, Don? It's Dimpy and Barbara. We're worried about you. Are you okay?"

Still no answer.

"Is the door open?" Barbara asked.

I tried the doorknob and shook my head. "It's locked."

"I have a master key," Barbara said, digging into one of her pockets. Once found, she used it to open the door and walk into the room while I followed, shutting it behind me.

We almost tripped over Don who lay on the floor at the foot of the bed. Guttural sounds came from his throat, and blood dripped from his nose.

On my knees beside him, trying not to panic, and in my most reassuring manner, I said, "Hold tight Don, help is on its way."

Barbara used her mobile to ring the ambulance and spoke into her phone with a forceful manner, no doubt relaying the urgency of the situation.

Blood dribbled from Don's mouth and his nose onto the carpet. His body had begun to shake, so I took a clean tissue from my blouse pocket and used it to wipe his face.

"Hang in there, Don. The ambulance will be here soon."

"Is that you, Dimpy?" Don asked, his voice reedy and slow.

"Yes, it's me ... and Barbara's here, too."

This seemed to register with him. With an effort, he grabbed hold of my arm. "Geez, Dimpy, I have a huge friggin' headache." Globules of blood fell from his mouth as he tried to cough.

Heart thumping and throat dry, my voice trembled as I looked at Barbara. "Where are those paramedics? He's getting worse."

"I'll keep an eye out for the ambulance while you wait with Don," Barbara said as she walked over to the door.

After what seemed an eternity while I held Don's hand and used tissues to wipe the blood that kept forming on his lips, Barbara poked her head in the door. "They're coming up the corridor now."

The paramedics wasted no time, as they burst through the open doorway, rummaged through bags and bent to examine Don.

"It's okay, buddy," one said as a groan escaped from Don's lips. "You'll be sorted in a jiffy."

Then it occurred to me with so many people in the room the paramedics would have trouble finding space to deal with Don. The doctor had also arrived, and Barbara was bringing him up to date on Don's condition. The room had become even more crowded.

With a little effort, I pushed myself to my feet and backed into the kitchenette. The tissue I had used to wipe Don's face was still in my hand. I flicked the rubbish lid up with my foot. Inside were some empty cans of beer and crushed up potato chip packets. I dropped the tissue on top and looked through the door to where the doctor and paramedics were still working on Don.

With my eyes focused on him, I inched forward to see what they were doing. Next moment, I staggered into a paramedic who held a stretcher in front of him, ready to place on the carpet. In the flurry of arms and stretcher, I tripped over and stumbled forwards. Horrified, I realised I was heading towards Don. To crash into him in his perilous state would be disastrous.

Barbara saved the day. She grabbed my arm and hauled me to an upright, stable position. "Dimpy, try to be more careful."

However, I wasn't listening. I recalled seeing a paramedic cut Don's tee-shirt open as I backed into the kitchenette. Now, at the height of my fall, I noticed the doctor was busy using a stethoscope on Don's chest. I'd also became aware of something which made little sense – Don's chest was covered in bruises.

This was puzzling. Barbara tapped me on the shoulder as I bent over to ask the doctor what might have caused them. "Dimpy," she said in a loud voice to get my attention.

I turned and faced her. "What is it?"

"Ronni rang me from the dining room. They saw the paramedics' hurry past, followed by the doctor and realised Don must be in trouble." Her bottom lip trembled, but after taking a deep breath, she continued speaking. "The paramedics need more room to attend to Don so she will be here soon to take you back to the dining room for a cup of tea."

"Or something stronger," I mumbled, thinking of the bottle of whiskey back in my apartment.

# Chapter 20

With extreme care, I negotiated my way to the door without falling over anyone. Ronni met me in the corridor outside Don's room, and we hugged each other.

"Where is Judith?" I asked.

"It's Dianne's birthday. She's spending the afternoon with the family before having dinner at a fancy restaurant."

We left Barbara to deal with the medics and headed back along the corridor towards the dining room.

Mrs B stood and watched us from the rec room doorway as we passed by. Did I imagine she had a triumphant grin on her face? A sudden thought came to my mind. The old witch must hope this meant a patio room would soon become vacant.

I joined Ronni at the dining room door and followed her inside, assuming we would be on our lonesome when we entered. It was a surprise to see about a dozen residents still seated at tables in the room.

News travels fast at the Manor, and Don's illness had been no exception. They talked in whispers among themselves as we came into the room. From the anxious looks on their faces; they had stayed with a hope there would be an update on Don's condition.

But it was impossible to do so because deep inside, I knew

Don would not survive; there seemed to be too much damage. And I had not had a chance to ask about the bruises.

Daisy tapped me on the shoulder. "Do you still want your lunch, Dimpy?"

"No, thank you. It was kind of you to keep it for me, but I am too upset to eat anything right now."

Daisy nodded and went back to the kitchen.

"What's wrong, Dimpy, is it Don? Is he going to be all right?" someone asked.

Neither Ronni nor I had much in the way of any news to impart. The only answer I could give them was that Barbara and I found Don lying on the floor of his room vomiting blood. The paramedics and his doctor were with him and doing everything possible to keep him alive.

Ronni brought a cup of tea to where I sat. "Do you suppose he is going to be okay?" she asked, placing the cup and saucer in front of me.

"I don't think so."

"Any idea what happened? I mean his getting ill seemed so sudden?"

"No, not a clue. At the moment I don't think anyone knows, not even the doctor."

However, I couldn't rid myself of the feeling of having missed something I'd seen or heard, and it was important.

My mind kept running around and around in my head, trying to remember what had happened since Don became ill. Deep in thought, I took a sip of tea.

"Dimpy, is something the matter?" Ronni's anxious voice got through to me.

I came to my senses again with a start. "Sorry Ronni, no, only in a daydream." It was time to give my thoughts rest, and maybe the memory would return of its own accord.

Mrs B must have come into the room behind us. She sat in

her usual seat by the door and had swivelled around to face us. In front of her body, she clasped the cane in a firm grip. Her scowl seemed to have disappeared. I thought this strange. Without her stern countenance, she looked almost happy. But why was she so happy? The only answer must be Don's unexpected illness.

Thoughts of Mrs B disappeared when Barbara appeared at the dining-room door. Everyone's head turned towards her as she entered the room. With a subdued look, she walked over to where Ronni and I sat and turned to face everyone.

"Can I have everybody's attention, please? There is sad news for you all." In a quiet and restrained manner, she said. "Don died a short while ago. The paramedics and the doctor did everything possible but could not save his life."

A low murmur ran through the group, and they stared at each other with hollow, shocked expressions.

Ronni and I looked at each other in dismay and burst into tears. Even though I'd seen the dreadful state Don had been in and thought he wouldn't recover, this news was still unexpected. He's always been the one we could turn to when we needed help. But now ... dead?

Mrs B made the first move. She rose from her chair near the door, and clutching her cane in her right hand, left the room without a word. Bang, shuffle, shuffle, bang, shuffle, shuffle.

Barbara raised her voice to be heard above Mrs B's clatter and explained because Don's death had been unusual, the police had been informed.

## Chapter 21

Ronni and I walked down the corridor to our separate apartments in silence. In the corridor, we stood near the wall with heads bowed while Don's covered body came past on a stretcher. He would be taken by ambulance to the mortuary for an autopsy, always a routine procedure for sudden unexplained death.

"I'm concerned about leaving you by yourself," Ronni said when we reached my apartment.

"I'll be fine, Ronni," I assured her as I opened my door. "Being alone to grieve would be the best thing to do at the moment." She stared at me for a few minutes but without saying anything more, turned and left as I closed the door behind her.

Tears ran down my face as I plucked tissues from a packet on the bedside table. I sat in my recliner and wept. Although we were all getting old, two deaths in a few weeks seemed unbearable at the moment. Don had been a good friend, and I would miss him. The little prickle inside me, which seemed to say I had overlooked something important was still there. Something significant had occurred about Don's death, but my memory refused to cooperate.

In the ensuite, I washed my face and combed my hair. Straightening my clothes, I walked to the laundry. My washing was dry, so I took it back to my room, folded it and put everything away in the wardrobe.

A check of my watch showed it was close to teatime, so I strolled to the dining room in case anybody had more news about Don. A sad lot of residents had gathered there for tea. Even Mrs B had not thumped and banged her cane as loudly as usual on her way to the dining room ahead of me.

Ronni joined me at a table, and we picked at our soup and sandwiches before all eyes veered to the door when Barbara appeared. She walked to the entrance to the kitchen and turned to face the room full of people. Molly and Daisy poked their heads out of the kitchen doorway and watched in silence.

With red and swollen eyes, her voice sounded gravelly as she spoke. "Sorry to disturb you. As you are aware, the past couple of weeks have not been pleasant for any of us. You are all aware Don died in unusual circumstances this afternoon." She coughed and cleared her throat and continued speaking. "The police have rung me to say his funeral will be held up for a while because a full post-mortem will need to be conducted, followed by an inquest. I will tell you the results as soon as I know myself."

People began to talk together in low voices. Barbara rapped her knuckles on the bench. "I haven't finished what I was saying yet." She paused until we all looked at her again. "With all this sadness from both Don and Barry's deaths, we need some cheering up. I have spoken with the Board of Management, and we agreed that early next month would be a good time for a break. There will be a special bus trip to the Hobart Botanical Gardens. It is coming to the end of spring, but the bulbs will still be in flower, and the roses are blooming." She paused and gave a weak smile before continuing, "This will be a free trip for anyone who would like to go. The Manor will supply a picnic lunch to eat while listening to the Hobart Symphony Orchestra.

This will be the first of the concerts they are performing in the gardens this year."

Everyone remained quiet when she finished speaking.

I stood up. "Thank you for telling us what is happening with Don. It is good of you and the Board to organise the trip and I, for one, will be going."

Barbara nodded to me, and as she walked out the door, the atmosphere seemed to become a little lighter.

## Chapter 22

Five days had gone by since Don passed away. I sat by myself in the reception area staring through the glass doors at the outside world, not sure what to do. I could either stick around in case the hospital rang Barbara with the result of Don's autopsy or take the bus to Launceston for a window-shopping expedition.

Although there had been a mild chill in the air early in the day, it had gradually warmed up, and now the sun shone in the cloudless sky, ideal for being outdoors. Ronni and Judith made the decision easy when they found me.

"We're going to have lunch in the city before going to the movies," Ronni said as she and Judith tapped me on the shoulder. "There's a good film being shown at the Ozone theatre this afternoon. We would like you to come with us."

She had brought today's newspaper with her, which she waved in front of my face. "The film's called 'Red Dog'. The critic says it's an excellent Australian movie."

"Yes," Judith said, chiming in. "Carol is coming, too. It'll be fun." She added: "and it'll give everyone something else to think about besides the dreadful things happening here."

We decided to meet in the reception area at 11.15 a.m. I returned to my room to change into grey trousers, ankle-high black boots and a cute woollen mauve jumper with two purple and white pompoms at the neckline. I slung a matching purple and white striped pashmina around my shoulders. A quick brush of my hair and a dab of lipstick and I was ready to go.

There was time to spare, so I strolled to the rec room and made a mug of strong coffee. For the past few nights, I had not slept well. Nightmares kept waking me up. My dreams returned time after time to Don's apartment and the way his body had bled. What could have caused all the bruises? Even his vomit had been black.

As I walked along the corridor to the reception area to meet my friends, my mobile phone rang. "It's Barbara here, where are you?" a voice said when I answered.

"In the corridor heading for the reception area. Ronni, Judith, Carol and I are going into town for lunch and watch a movie."

"I thought you might like to know Constable McKellar rang a little while ago. Sometime today Sergeant Plate is calling into the Manor to discuss the results of Don's autopsy and inquest. Would you like me to let you know their findings when you get back?"

"Thanks, Barbara, that would be great. We should be home about five o'clock, and I look forward to hearing the outcome and what steps if any the police intend to take."

Ronni had called a taxi to pick us up at eleven-thirty. It drew up in front of the entrance to the Manor right on time and waited for us to board. Because of her bulk, Carol would sit next to the driver. This left more room in the back for us.

As we went through the main door, my big feet once again got me into trouble. I tripped over Sergeant Plate as he came up the steps towards me, reading a piece of paper and not looking where he was going. Carol had been chatting to me about her comfortable new bed, so I had not seen him.

Well, that's not one hundred per cent true. I glimpsed the sergeant's somewhat squat figure out the corner of my eye, which gave me enough time to extend my arm in a more or less defensive gesture. Unfortunately, I poked him in the face with my fingers. There came a shrill yelp as he took several quick steps backwards which, to my dismay, caused him to stumble and stagger sideways into a large pot plant that stood to one side of the entrance door. The sergeant lay flat on his back on top of the plant. Words escaped me. Embarrassment flooded my face like a tsunami; my cheeks felt as if they were on fire.

Judith, Ronni and Carol stood transfixed. They resembled store dummies, and stared at the policeman, as he struggled to his feet. Even the taxi driver, head poking out the window, had watched it happen. His tight lips compressed into a line, which meant he was trying hard not to laugh.

Picking himself up and dusting the back of his trousers, Sergeant Plate's eyes met mine, a wry smile on his lips. "I guessed it was you, Dimpy."

Next to the taxi, my friends stood laughing their heads off.

"I'm sorry," I blurted out "This seems to have become a habit … bumping into each other, I mean."

Sergeant Plate gave me another ironic smile. "In future, I'll try to stay out of your way." Then, as an afterthought, he added, "In fact, I am beginning to think you're downright dangerous. Now, if you will excuse me …"

But I couldn't let it rest there. "Please, Sergeant Dish – er Plate, before you go, can you tell me anything at all about what happened to Don. Above all, what caused his death?"

Without answering my direct question and in mid-step, he said, "I'm here to brief Ms Wakefield, about the outcome from Mr Aha … er, Don's autopsy. It's up to her to tell you the results."

With a curt nod, he strode through the front door and disappeared into Barbara's office. It looked as though I would have to wait until later for answers to the questions. The taxi driver beeped his horn, and I hurried over to the ladies who were seated in the taxi waiting for me.

I assumed the autopsy results would show what I had suspected all along. Don had been murdered.

# Chapter 23

As Ronni had predicted, lunch in town had been fun with lots of laughter and reminiscences. We pushed Don's death to the back of our minds for a little while. The movie finished shortly before five o'clock.

A cold breeze had sprung up while we were inside the theatre. It made me shiver, so I pulled the pashmina closer around my body. The sun had begun to dip behind the Western Tiers. Spring was here, but darkness still descended in the late afternoons. The taxi, ordered in advance, arrived not long after we came out of the cinema. We piled in, grateful for its warmth.

After it dropped us near the front entrance to the Manor, Ronni did the honours and paid our fares.

Judith stopped on the bottom of the steps and asked. "Who's the person standing in the doorway? They seem to be waiting for something or someone."

By narrowing my eyes, I made out a figure at the main entrance, lit by a light shining from above the door. It did not take me long to make out who stood there. Barbara Wakefield. At work, she wore her hair in a neat bun which now stood out in the shadows. By the way she rocked backwards and forwards on the balls of her feet and stared into the growing darkness, something bothered her.

"Yes, it's Barbara," I replied. "She must be waiting for us. I wonder what's happened while we were away?" I took a deep breath and walked across to where she stood. She had mentioned earlier on the phone there might be news about Don's autopsy. Sergeant Plates visit earlier in the day would have been about that.

Barbara came down the steps towards me. "Sorry to be a nuisance Dimpy," she said when she realised it was me. "Before you left, you told me you would be out for lunch and then at the movies but would be home about this time. I decided to wait here because I was anxious to let you know the results of Don's autopsy."

"We would all like to know," Ronni said, as she, Carol and Judith came and stood next to me.

"Okay. The report has shown Don's system was overloaded with Warfarin." We were silent for a moment while she took a deep breath and continued: "A horrendous quantity of the drug was found in his system. Enough to kill two men. No wonder his nose bled, and his body was covered with purple blotches."

As we talked, the evening became colder. Judith had begun to shiver, and the pashmina I wore was not warm enough to stop the cold seeping into my bones. I indicated with a nod for my friends to go past us into the Manor. I would discuss the results of our talk on the front step with them later. Besides, it was teatime, and Carol would not be happy if she missed out on her sandwiches and cake.

I turned back to Barbara. "But Warfarin is a blood thinner," I said. "Don took tablets for high blood pressure, but he never mentioned his blood needed thinning."

"This afternoon, Constable McKellar did a complete check the same as she did with Barry's medication. Don had not been prescribed Warfarin by the doctor."

"Where did Don get the pills? If his doctor didn't prescribe them, did somebody give them to him?"

"After Sergeant Plate left, I spent some time during the afternoon, asking several residents the same question."

I explained how close-knit Don had become to Ronni, Judith and me. Taking Warfarin without telling anybody did not sound like the Don we knew.

"Yes, it's obvious you were close. However –" Barbara began to say.

Another thought came to my mind. "You have to have regular blood checks if you're on Warfarin. Your staff would have queried the medication when they gave out his tablets?"

As Barbara mulled the idea over, I hurried on. "If that's the case, then Don couldn't have been taking them. Blood thinners would mean regular trips to the clinic for testing. Don never went there unless he felt desperately ill or needed a new prescription." She still did not look convinced. "He spent most days hanging around with his mates either at the Ball and Chain pub or the bowls club. The fact is if Don so much as blinked, one of us would have known about it."

Turning toward me, Barbara placed a hand on my arm. "Come inside with me, Dimpy. We need to make a phone call."

"Who to?"

"Sergeant Plate, who else. Being his best friend, I'm sure Don would have told you if he was taking Warfarin. Before making any more decisions about how Don died, he needs to talk to you."

We moved into Barbara's office and phoned the police station. The constable who answered the phone told us Sergeant Plate would be in Hobart for a few days attending to two trial dates. The sergeant would return as soon as possible and would be in touch when he arrived back at the Kinross Police Station.

After parting ways with Barbara, I continued down the corridor to the dining room. Ronni and Judith sat at a table eating their food and chatting to each other when I walked in.

Their curious eyes turned towards me as I collected a plate of sandwiches from the buffet table, made a cup of tea and joined them. Carol was nowhere in sight. She had finished her meal and went back to her room. "She was tired after our day out and said she would catch up on the news about Don some other time," Ronnie said.

I told them about the rest of my talk with Barbara, and they both shook their heads.

"No, I'm sure Don had not been taking Warfarin," Judith said. "My view is that Don was killed, and the murderer somehow forced him to take the tablets."

"A trifle fanciful, Judith," Ronni replied. "The results of the autopsy sound suspicious, but his death may also be accidental. It's no use jumping to conclusions."

My mind was in a muddle. I found it difficult enough to believe Don had died, and harder still to think somebody hated him so much they killed him. However, it would be better to keep my thoughts to myself. At least until Barbara and I had an interview with Sergeant Plate. We needed to know what conclusions the police had made about Don's death.

## Chapter 24

A few days later, Barbara came to my room after breakfast and knocked on the door. I was making the bed and reflected it was time to complete my latest novella. After a final edit, the manuscript could be ready to email to the publisher that afternoon. All thoughts of the story fled when she cleared her throat.

"Constable McKellar has rung back to let us know Sergeant Plate would like to see us at the police station at 11 o'clock this morning," she said before I could say hello. "Is it okay with you, Dimpy?"

"Yes, of course."

"Good. It's beginning to rain so we will take my car. See you at the front entrance at quarter to eleven."

Barbara was waiting in her car when I walked down the front steps of the Manor. A persistent drizzle of rain made it difficult to find a park near our destination. However, luck was on our side for a change. A utility across from the police station drove out from where he had parked, and we slotted straight in.

At the police station, a young desk officer ushered us into an office where Sergeant Plate stood behind a desk. As we walked into the room, he nodded to two chairs Constable McKellar was placing on the other side of the desk facing him. We sat while Constable McKellar drew up a chair nearer to a wall.

We described the Don we had known well, and how unlikely it was he'd have taken Warfarin without our knowledge. Both officers listened without interrupting and nodded now and then, as if interested in what we had to say.

The rain pelted down, the drumming on the roof a loud background noise in the office. An oil heater turned to high, was set against a wall near the door, but the heat made the room stuffy.

In a firm voice, I said, "Both Barbara and I are certain Don and Barry were murdered. Mind you, as yet we have no proof, only female intuition."

Sergeant Plate sat back in his chair, both hands clasped across his belly and nodded his head. "Most interesting," he replied. "Thank you for providing more information. Every little bit helps in this kind of situation."

*This kind of situation?* I was astounded, finding it hard to believe his choice of words. Did he mean Don's death was not from natural causes or murder? I turned to Barbara to confirm what he said. She looked as stunned as me. Her eyes had a shocked look, and her bottom lip dropped. However, she was the first to recover.

A managerial firmness sounded in her voice, "What do you mean by *situation*?" she inquired, glaring at the sergeant. "Do you mean he committed suicide?"

With the back of his hand, he half pointed, half waved towards Constable McKellar. "She will explain it to you."

Constable McKellar shifted about in her seat as she fumbled with her notebook. After a few deep breaths, she looked at us and began a hesitant explanation.

"As you are both aware, we have received the autopsy report from the hospital, which shows Mr Ahegge's death had been caused by … um … an overdose of Warfarin. It's probable Mr Ahegge may have contributed to his death. That's what the evidence suggests, and so our investigation is now finalised. A full report has been forwarded to the coroner."

"What did the coroner have to say?" Barbara asked.

"He has deemed the death to be caused by Mr Ahegge's own hand. Now the case is closed." She shut her notebook and looked directly at us. In a low, sorrowful voice, she murmured, "We understand Mr Ahegge's funeral will be held next week. His son will advise the Manor of the exact details."

Sergeant Plate shrugged with open hands at us. "Now ladies, Constable McKellar has explained the situation to you. Let's leave it at that, shall we."

With an incredulous look of indignant disbelief, I shook my head and stared back at him.

"I can see you're upset," the sergeant said. "It's natural. Suicide, when it involves someone close, is always hard to accept." He pushed his chair back and rose to his full height of five feet odd. "However, accept it we must, so ladies, if you'll excuse us ..."

Not prepared to leave it there I said, "You can't be serious. Don was a loveable, carefree guy. Why would he want to do away with himself?" I turned to Barbara who, by the quizzical tilt of her head and upturned eyelashes, also looked amazed by what he had told us

"Yes," she said in a no-nonsense voice, "the allegation is ridiculous. As we explained, Dimpy and I understood Don like the back of our hands. There's no way he'd take his own life."

"Sometimes we don't understand people as well as we believe we do," Sergeant Plate said. "I've seen evidence time and time again of this kind of thing happening. As he was your friend, I do sympathise with you."

"Stop patronising us," I snapped, "the decision is wrong."

Sergeant Plate's next words were like a slap in the face. "I hoped not to mention this because the information involves one of your own, but new evidence came to light during the past few days, which led us to this conclusion."

Barbara sat forward and in her best demanding voice said, "By one of your own, I take it you mean someone at the Manor?"

"Yes, one of your residents has come forward with valuable information related to Mr Ahegge's death."

"Oh? And who might they be?" I asked.

"We are not at liberty to say. The person concerned was present during an argument between the deceased and his son, David." He picked up a paper from the desk and scanned it. "Our informant told us Don's son became upset because he claimed the stocks in which his father invested were decreasing in value. He pleaded with his father to instruct his stockbroker to sell them." He replaced the piece of paper on the desk, sat back and looked at us. "The situation became heated. Mr Ahegge told his son he was sick of arguing and determined to end it once and for all."

A sudden chill cascaded through my body. The sergeants' tone and message had not escaped me "No," I said with conviction, fighting to defeat the sudden quiver in my voice. "You've got it wrong. Don didn't mean he wanted to do away with himself. No, he would have intended to solve the problem in some other way." I took a deep breath before continuing, "Furthermore, why would Don have come to lunch the day he died complaining about illness? He had been his usual cheerful self at breakfast. Laughing and joking with everyone as usual. It would make no sense to act that way if he intended to commit suicide."

I looked across at Barbara, hoping for support. Before she could react, the sergeant said, "We're very sorry, ladies. We know how much you cared about Mr Ahegge."

Because the noise of the rain on the roof made it difficult to hear Sergeant Plate's voice, we leaned forward in our chairs.

He raised his voice and continued. "The son has confirmed this was the conversation the witness overheard between himself and his father. So, after all the information had been presented, the coroner concluded that Mr Donald Ahegge took his own life."

My stomach churned, and nausea rose into my throat and stung my nostrils. With sudden rage, I flew to my feet, skittling the chair behind me, leant towards Sergeant Plate inches from his nose and shook my fist. "Listen to me … you can't friggin' assume …"

Thank goodness, Barbara pulled me back into my seat and stopped me before I could say more. A hand squeezed my shoulder. "Leave it, Dimpy," she said. Her voice sounded sad and tired as she continued. "It's time to go. They're not listening to us."

As I stood up, my legs shook. Straightening to my full height, I nodded bleakly to both Sergeant Plate and Constable McKellar. Tears filled my eyes as I marched out of the room. Barbara caught up with me at the front counter, and we left the police station together.

"I don't care what they believe," I said when we sat in the car. "There is something horrible happening at the Manor, and we must get to the bottom of it before there's another death."

Barbara started the car and drove out into the traffic. My tears fell in a steady stream, matched by the continual drumming of rain on the roof.

## Chapter 25

On Wednesday morning after Barbara and I visited the police station, the painting class was hard at work in the rec room. I had spent Tuesday afternoon thinking about the discussion with the police officers about Don's death. On the way home from the police station, we'd agreed not to tell anyone of our suspicions that Barry and Don were murdered. Instead, we would keep eyes and ears out for any sign of unrest or sudden illness among the residents or staff.

As a young girl during the Depression years, my mother had been an artist, and one job she held was painting roses onto lampshades. She liked to draw studies of flowers in detail and stored them all in scrapbooks until she became too ill to hold a brush. There are two paintings of miniature roses hanging on the wall behind my bed, both painted by my mother. One is of pink roses in full bloom, and the other shows yellow roses coming into bud. More of her paintings were kept in a drawer inside my wardrobe.

Pictures on the wall painted by me would never happen. I did not inherit an art gene or a musical one, but Judith loves the art sessions. She had the knack of painting still-life pictures of tables with bowls of fruit on them.

"Painting still-life became easy for me because as a young

child, most of the presents I received on my birthday and for Christmas were drawings called 'painting by numbers'. There was a different number for each colour, so over time they became easy to paint."

She confided this to me one day after her eighth painting appeared on a wall in her room. They were all the same style of picture, painted in various colours, depending on her Picasso or Rembrandt mood.

After tidying my apartment, I walked to the local shop across from the park and brought the newspaper. Back in my room, I made a coffee and sat in the recliner to do the crosswords and cryptogram.

As I folded the paper to put in the recycle bin, a knock came on the door, and a voice called out, "Are you there, Dimpy? It's Judith."

"Come in," I shouted back, and she opened the door and stood there, juggling another masterpiece under her arm. She still wore her painting smock.

The pinafore covered her from neck to knee. I hoped she had remembered to put clothes on underneath; as apart from a couple of ties, it was open at the back. Splotches of paint were splattered on both sleeves and front of the smock she wore. There was also some blue paint specks in her hair.

"While I was passing, I decided to call in and let you know Don's funeral will be held next Monday," she said, clamping a firm grip on the painting with both hands as it tried to slip out of her grasp. "While our class was in progress, Barbara put two announcements on the notice board. One is the details about Don's funeral, and the other is information for the trip to the Botanical Gardens on Tuesday of the following week. I have put my name on both lists."

"Thanks for letting me know. As its near lunchtime I'll put my name down before going into the dining room," I replied, concerned she would drop the painting. "But first, do you need any help carrying your picture?"

"No, it's okay," she said, giving the painting a final hitch up under her arm as she shuffled sideways into the corridor. "Next time Dianne drops in for a visit, she will hang it for me. Bye."

After rising from my chair and going over to shut the door behind her, I sighed with relief. Yes, she wore a skirt and jumper under the smock.

Ronni had gone out straight after breakfast to join some friends for a shopping trip in the city and would not be back until teatime. Perhaps after Don's funeral might be a good time for a discussion with her about how badly Todd was treating his mother. Maybe together, we could think of a way to stop it happening in the future.

I brushed my hair in the bathroom mirror, put on some lipstick and decided to drop into the rec room straight away. Still thinking about Todd, I almost forgot to put on shoes instead of slippers but remembered when I opened the door.

The lists were on the noticeboard outside the rec room. Yes, Don's funeral would be held next Monday commencing at 11.00 am at the local funeral home. According to the notice, his son, David Brown, had invited everyone from the Manor to attend the service. A burial would follow at the town cemetery. After the service, we were welcome to join the family at the local hotel to drink a toast to David's father.

We never heard much about the son because Don had not been pleased with him for changing his name to Brown. I was still not happy about his interview with the police. No matter what anyone else thought, I was not prepared to accept that his father had taken his own life. I entered my name in the space provided for people attending the funeral.

Don had once mentioned his son owned a hardware shop in Hobart. Browns Hardware Store sounded better and was easier to pronounce than Ahegge's Hardware Store. But Brown? From one extreme to another, I thought.

Then I signed up for the trip to the Botanical Gardens. After a moment I decided to write Ronni's name on both lists, confident she would want to come along to both the funeral and Botanical Gardens.

Although the Botanical Gardens list was filling fast, there were not as many names for the funeral. Don had seemed popular with the many of the residents of the Manor. Although a few people had objected to his swearing and heavy drinking. On occasions, some people had complained to Barbara about his language. When contacted by the Board of Management and asked to stop, he always apologised to everyone. However, after a while, he would be back to his old ways again.

I was right about the funeral service. On Monday morning, apart from myself, Ronni, Judith, Barbara, Daisy and, of course, Mrs B, only six other residents walked to the funeral parlour.

"Molly's in charge of the kitchen, and busy making cold meat and salad for lunch, and there's jellied fruit in the refrigerator for sweets," Daisy told me on the way there.

"You like Molly, don't you?"

"Yes, I do. She is such a good worker, and everyone likes her pleasant personality. She makes people laugh at the funny things she says."

About to enquire what she meant by "funny things", I kept my mouth closed and decided not to ask.

As we entered the funeral parlour, I asked Barbara if she needed help to move Don's belongings from his patio apartment.

"No Dimpy, I rang his son, and he's bringing a few of Don's friends here tomorrow afternoon to sort through everything. They intend giving most of his clothes and other bits and pieces to the local op shop."

I grinned, imagining the op shop ladies holding up a heap of well-worn singlets, shorts and sandals and wondering what to do with them.

"Are you all right, Dimpy?"

"Yes, Barbara," I replied coming back to earth with a thump. "I remembered how Don's language used to cause such a stir."

"Yes, he could be a friggin' pain in the neck at times."

We both laughed, and it lightened the mood a little as I prepared myself for another unwelcome funeral service.

When we entered the funeral home, meeting Don's son was a bit of a shock because he looked like a younger image of his father, right down to the pot belly. He was dressed in a suit, of course, not shorts and sandals. He kept scuffing his shoes and fiddling with his shirt collar, which made me guess this was not his usual way of dressing.

We introduced ourselves to him, and his wife and exchanged commiserations. Two of his eldest children were also present. Bite your tongue, Dimpy, I decided, and don't make problems by initiating an embarrassing argument with Don's son about his father's supposed suicide.

Don's old friends from the pub were also present and looked self-conscious in suits and ties.

After a short eulogy and two hymns, we all walked the half a kilometre to the graveyard. With a sense of loss, Ronni, Judith and I sobbed as we watched the coffin lowered into the ground.

We said goodbye to Don's son and family after the cemetery and caught a bus back to the Manor. None of the residents, including Mrs B, had felt like going to the hotel for what we were sure would be a boozy wake.

Because the funeral had been late in the morning, we missed lunch. After deliberating, we caught the local bus into the city for a late meal at a café and an afternoon of window shopping.

Ronni needed a new toothbrush and hair conditioner, and we all needed new library books.

We arrived back at the Manor before teatime. As I walked to my room, a memory came to me. I had meant to talk to Ronni about Judith's son, Todd. After mulling it over, I decided to leave it until after Todd's next visit to his mother in case his behaviour towards her had improved, but I feared the worst.

# Chapter 26

A warm, sunny day dawned for our bus trip to the Hobart Botanical Gardens. It was just over a week since Don's funeral and life at the Manor had begun to return to normal.

Yesterday had become another good news day when Barbara advised Ronni the vacant patio apartment would be hers. She had to wait for a few days while the apartment was repainted, and a new carpet installed. Such excitement as the Manor groundsmen moved and settled her belongings into their new home.

"Because both Barry and Don were my friends, it saddens me, Dimpy, but perhaps they would have liked the fact it's me moving in and not Mrs B."

Barbara had hired a big bus which held forty-eight people. Carol, of course, needed two seats to accommodate her bulk, which left forty-six seats available for other residents and staff.

As we waited for the bus to arrive, it was nice to see so many people with smiles on their faces again. Everybody seemed determined to leave the sadness of Barry and Don's deaths behind and enjoy themselves. The TV weatherman had predicted a warm and sunny spring day, perfect for a picnic.

Nearly all the residents had opted to enjoy a free day out. When the bus pulled up outside the entrance to the Manor,

Daisy became busy counting picnic baskets and checking the contents before the driver loaded them into the storage area.

"Where's Molly?" I asked her while standing in line waiting to board.

"She's staying behind to make sure anybody not going on the trip has a decent lunch. However, it looks as if there will only be for a few people to feed. Our tea will be ready for us as soon as we arrive home." She sighed with contentment. "Molly is a capable little soul. Today is the first time I've come on a bus trip; confident everything will be organised for when we return home."

Barbara looked pleased with the response to the trip. When the bus arrived, she sat in a front seat next to me. "There's a happy atmosphere around us," I said. "Everyone is looking forward to a change of scenery."

Barbara grinned as she pointed to Mrs B, who was busy, organising herself and her massive handbag in a front seat opposite us. To allow a new resident, Julie Mathison, to sit next to her, she had, with a great deal of apparent reluctance, moved a few centimetres closer to the window.

"Isn't there somewhere else you can sit?" Mrs B scowled and muttered.

"I'm sorry," Julie replied, "all the other seats are taken."

With her mouth set in a downward pout, Mrs B turned her head towards the window and ignored Julie, who shrugged, pulled a book out of her handbag and began to read.

"Nobody received a tick this morning," Barbara said with a chuckle, "because Mrs B was much too busy gobbling breakfast as fast as possible. She wanted to make sure to be the first person on the bus and bag a front seat." She gazed across the aisle to where Mrs B sat.

"It's evident by her behaviour towards Julie she expected to have it all to herself."

"Thanks to your quick-thinking Barbara, this trip became important to almost everybody. It will be good for us to relax and not worry about death for a while."

"Yes. If this outing is successful, we could run more trips in the future."

Barbara looked around and began counting heads. "We're all accounted for and ready to leave," she said in a loud voice to the bus driver.

As the bus pulled out from the Manor, she turned to me. "While I listened to the chatter around the Manor during the past week, it's obvious most of the residents still consider Don and Barry's deaths to be suspicious."

"Me too," I said. "Perhaps, in this case, the police investigations could have been more thorough."

"You may be right about that," Barbara said before opening a folder which lay on her lap and beginning to read.

The drive to Hobart would take over three hours, but I'd come prepared and brought a magazine to read. As I flipped the pages, there was a tap on my shoulder. Ronni, who was sitting with Judith in the seat behind me, leaned over and whispered, "Watch out for Mrs B today because she's in a foul mood."

About to say she was always unpleasant and nasty, I decided to hold my tongue. Today was supposed to be a day for happy thoughts, not one for worrying about cranky old ladies.

Nevertheless, I made a point of avoiding eye contact with Mrs B when we all trooped off the bus for a toilet and morning tea break halfway to Hobart. Everyone, including the driver, tucked into thermoses of tea and coffee plus three different types of slices made by Daisy and Molly.

Judith sat on a bench next to Ronni to eat her morning tea. I hoped she had overheard the warning about Mrs B. Although with Judith's state of mind, even if she had known earlier about her grumpy mood, she could well have forgotten.

Mrs B, face scrunched up and grim, thumped down next to her and began giving a bemused and speechless Judith a proper tongue lashing; holding onto her stick with one hand and jabbing at Judith's chest with the other, ranting on about the patio rooms being shared among friends and not residents like herself.

"Leave Judith alone, you horrible mean woman," an indignant Ronni declared in a loud voice. "I'm the one you should be talking to, not Judith. Friendship was not an issue because my name come up next on the list for a patio apartment. You will have to wait for your turn."

Taken aback, Mrs B stood up, stomped over to the bus and waited for the door to open.

When we all climbed aboard for the second half of the journey, I noticed Mrs B was smiling. It was a thin, sour smile as if she knew something we didn't, which was a worry. Mrs B could be a nasty piece of work.

Determined not to let her spoil my day, I dismissed her from my mind and returned to gazing out the window. Either from the steady drone of the bus or the fact that most of the other passengers were napping, I dozed off.

Barbara's voice woke me up. We had arrived at the gardens, and she was busy telling everyone to gather their things and disembark. The bus had pulled up in the small parking area outside the entrance gate. It was just after 11.30 am. We had made good time, and the sun still shone on our day out. Not a trace of a cloud in the sky.

Standing next to the bus, milling around with the rest of the passengers, I turned to Barbara. "What do we do now?" I asked.

Pointing into the open bus storage area and in her managerial voice, she addressed the group: "All those who can help, please grab a picnic basket or folding chair. The driver has offered to carry the eskies containing our lunches." She turned to him and continued, "Please take them to the grassed section in front of the orchestral area. It's not far from here."

With most of us carrying something, even those with walkers, we made our way into the Botanical Gardens. As we set ourselves up, we watched the busy orchestra members unfolding stools and checking their instruments. Men were installing a sound system on either side of the make-shift stage.

We had timed it well; the orchestra began tuning up as those who were able made themselves comfortable on rugs placed on the lawn. Those residents who had brought their walkers remained seated on them. Soon other members of the public began to arrive. Like us, most were carrying picnic rugs and snacks.

After a short while, we settled down to enjoy our sandwiches, slices and cups of tea or coffee while listening to the music, which began with excerpts from musical comedies.

Behind the musicians, we admired the view of the gardens and the river in the distance. We smelled the gentle fragrance from the Daphne bushes planted nearby. The sound of children playing games on the grass or fiddling with their phones came as a distant, muted background noise.

Barbara gave me a nudge. "After lunch and the concert," she whispered, "everyone can take a leisurely walk around the gardens. There are two hours to fill before the bus is ready to return to the Manor."

"Okay," I agreed, having visited the gardens before. "There's plenty to see. The Japanese garden, the hothouses and the vegetable patch are within an easy stroll from where we are now."

"Good idea, Dimpy. Everyone will enjoy the scenery and maybe get a chance to talk to the presenter from *Gardening Australia* if he's around somewhere in the grounds."

I pointed over my shoulder. "However, it's a steep climb up

the slope to see the Tasmanian native gardens. Most of our group wouldn't make it."

At the end of the concern, after the applause had died down, Barbara explained her plan to everyone. Those on walkers opted for the hothouses, veggie patch and gentle walks around the flower beds. There were a few who decided to stay behind, sit in the sun and chat or enjoy an after-dinner snooze.

Barbara had been right. The trip had been an ideal way to take our mind off Barry and Don's deaths. Although I would never forget the awful sight of Don surrounded by the paramedics as he lay dying on the floor of his apartment.

## Chapter 27

I accompanied Judith and Ronni to stroll around flower beds and the vegetable patch. Then we sat and watched as the orchestra loaded their instruments onto a truck and disconnected the sound system.

Judith sighed as she gazed up the hill. "I'd love to see the view from up there: all the Botanical Gardens, Government House and the Derwent River. However, I don't think I can walk up a steep uphill slope. Not even with the help of a walker."

Barbara, with the help of Daisy, was busy repacking the remains of the picnic into baskets and folding rugs into a pile. The bus driver helped by carrying the rubbish to the big bins dotted around the gardens.

"The kiosk at the bottom of the hill has wheelchairs for hire in case somebody might need one," Barbara remarked. "I read about them on the pamphlet the Botanical Gardens sent me when I told them we were coming." She turned to me and said, "I'm sure Dimpy would not mind pushing you up the hill."

Yes, being in a wheelchair would suit eighty-three-year-old Judith and her sparrow like frame. "I wonder if they have one left for me to use," Judith said hopefully.

"I'm full of food and too comfortable to move," Ronni told

us. "I am going to stay here and soak up the sun and perhaps take a short walk to the Japanese garden in a little while."

With Judith ensconced in a hired wheelchair, we strolled up the path, bituminised thank goodness, all the way to the top of the hill. When we reached the crest, I manoeuvred Judith's chair to the side of the path and onto a patch of grass. An excellent place to stop and look around.

"It's a nice view, with the gardens in the foreground and the river and mountains in the distance," Judith said after I helped her apply the brake on her chair.

"Yes, and with Mount Wellington behind us, overlooking Hobart, it sets the place off," I pointed down the hill, "And at the bottom of the hill behind those bushes, there's a pond. I hadn't noticed it before."

"No, it's hard to spot unless you are aware it's there. Look at those people walking from the kiosk along the path opposite the pond; they haven't noticed it either."

"It doesn't seem so. Those tall reeds growing on the edge plus big rocks surrounding the pond don't make it any easier, but I suppose they're there for a reason."

"Maybe they've been placed at the pond to stop people falling in," Judith suggested, as a young girl and boy climbed onto one of the larger rocks and threw scraps of bread into the water for the ducks. Several drifted out from a clump of reeds to inspect what awaited them. When they saw the bread, they flapped and skidded their way across the water towards the scraps amidst a great deal of quacking.

"Everyone's enjoying themselves," Judith said, gazing at the view and the people who walked along the paths around different parts of the garden. Children played tag, threw frisbees or turned somersaults on the lawns below us.

"They're having a great time. There's the stream with a miniature waterfall at the Japanese garden. It was my favourite place when I visited with my husband." A smile creased my face with the memory. "Among other things, there's the tiny bridge which spans the stream. The surroundings are so peaceful."

"After our run-in with Mrs B at Campbell Town, it sounds the perfect place for Ronni to visit and chill out before we go home," Judith said. "You can go on ahead down the path past the Tasmanian display, Dimpy. I would like to stay here for a little while longer to take in the view, then negotiating my way down the path and past the pond to the kiosk. And before you ask, yes, I'll be careful and take my time."

"Okay, if you are sure you will be all right?"

Judith nodded, so I scrambled down the path, looking right and left at the different trees and bushes as I passed by.

There came a sound of someone screaming. I turned and looked behind me to where I thought the noise had come from and glimpsed Judith as she hurtled down the path towards me in the wheelchair. Her arms waved in the air, her voice at full shriek, totally out of control.

With no time to think, I dived to the side of the path, tripped and knocked into a man sitting on a stone seat. The wheelchair came past, clipping my heel before continuing on its way.

"Oops, sorry," I apologised to the man, pushing myself back onto the path. Without pausing to take a breath, I charged down the hill behind the fast disappearing wheelchair.

The two children near the pond must have heard the screams. With startled looks, they jumped onto a rock then stood still as Judith swayed towards them. Without stopping, I shouted out to the girl and boy to get out of the friggin' way – several times. At the bottom of the hill, not heeding my frantic warnings, they stood as though frozen to the spot. What followed was a sight I'll always remember.

As the wheelchair flew past the two youngsters, their mouths gaped, and necks swivelled while they watched it crash headlong into the rock near where they stood.

Petticoat and dress ballooned, and arms flapped as Judith, with a splash, arrived at her eventual destination near the centre of the pond.

I continued to move down the hill as fast as my seventy plus-year-old body would allow and arrived in time to see her splashing about in the pond. Ducks, in a fury of feathers, swam past her with loud quacks.

Heart pounding from the terrible fright I received seeing Judith crash down the hill, it took a few moments before I could talk coherently.

"Judith! What happened? Are you okay? Did you knock the brake lever?" Could it have been her tiny frame that saved her from injury? I was not sure. As far as I could tell, she had survived intact. I was amazed when, without assistance and almost straight away, she made for the edge, half paddling, half wading.

When she reached the edge of the pond, she grabbed my outstretched hand. With care, one hand under her armpit for balance, I helped her climb out of the water onto one of the rocks. Water dripped from Judith's clothes, her hair plastered to her head, she half crawled, half scrambled up over the rest of the rocks and sat down on the path. The boy and girl still stood there, perhaps to check out the old lady who flew through the air before their eyes.

The wheelchair remained upside down but listed to one side where a wheel had buckled under the impact. Ducks surrounded it as they quacked and beat their wings with fright.

After negotiating the rocks, I pushed my way past the two children and helped Judith to her feet. "Are you okay? What on earth happened? Where do you hurt?"

"I think I'm okay. A bit shaky, a few cuts on the arms and

legs, and I'll have some big bruises tomorrow." She looked at the wheelchair and shook her head. "But I'm afraid the wheelchair is totalled."

One of the gardeners appeared, and between us, we helped Judith slowly limp over to a convenient seat. I thanked the man and told him we would be all right. He nodded, then waded into the pond, retrieved the wheelchair and left, holding it firmly off the ground with both hands. Although the seat was still okay, the rest of the chair was bent out of shape. I thought Judith had been lucky to have come away with only cuts and bruises.

Judith shivered as she sat on the seat, soaking wet, miserable and cold. Teeth chattering, she asked, "H, h, how on earth did I manage to end up in the duck pond, Dimpy?"

"I've no idea. I'd only meandered down the path for a few minutes when I heard someone screaming. When I looked behind me, you were coming towards me – racing down the hill on the wheelchair, which ended up in the pond looking a terrible mess. You were lucky to survive the fall."

"I can't understand why it happened," she mumbled.

I took Judith by the arm. "Let's go to the kiosk; they'll most likely have towels to rub you down. While we're at it, we should tell them they're now minus a working wheelchair."

"Dimpy," she said as I helped her limp along the footpath. "While I watched you continue down the hill, I felt a hand on the back of my neck. There came the sound of a chuckle." Judith took a deep breath. "I'm almost certain someone pushed me."

I stopped and turned to face her. "What? Are you sure? Wasn't the brake on?"

"I had just released it and was about to start wheeling slowly down the hill." She turned to me with tears in her eyes. "Oh, Dimpy, I'm afraid to say it, but do you think someone tried to kill me?"

"Don't be silly. Why would someone want to harm you?"

Barbara came racing along the path towards us. "Judith, are you all right? What happened? Are you hurt?" She gasped for breath and had to wait a few minutes before being able to talk again. "I was in the gift shop, and a lady came in and told me there had been an accident at the pond. She remembered seeing the lady involved sitting with our group listening to the music."

"I'm okay. A bit shook up." Judith looked ruefully at her wet clothes and shivered. "It will be a damp trip home. Not expecting to become wet, I didn't bring a change of clothes with me."

I hugged her. "It will be okay; We'll manage something".

Barbara turned as she heard her name called. Daisy came puffing up to her. "Here," she said, handing a blanket to Barbara. "After I heard about a problem at the duck pond, I raced back to our group and grabbed this from the back of one of the chairs in case Judith needed it."

"Thank you," Barbara said, taking the blanket from her and wrapping it around Judith. "We'll go to the ladies restroom in the kiosk and see what we can find to make you presentable and dry for the trip home."

The lady behind the desk in the kiosk gave us a surprised look as we walked in but was most helpful. Tut-tutting to herself after hearing Judith's story, she hurried away to find makeshift clothes from a 'left behind' box that might fit. She pointed to a room behind her. "You can get changed in our staffroom, love," she said, handing a towel and a pile of clothes across the counter. "These're not what you'd call elegant, but they'll keep you warm."

Judith dried herself properly and dressed in track pants, polo neck jumper which came down past her knees and a pair of well-worn fur-lined boots. Under her arm, she carried a parcel which contained her wet clothes.

Barbara asked the staff to arrange an invoice for the cost of the wheelchair. We thanked everyone at the kiosk for their help and made our way to where the bus was parked.

Barbara looked at her watch. "Most of the others are already on the bus now with all our belongings, so we can leave once I check everybody is aboard."

Judith and I were almost last onto the bus which, as you'd expect, buzzed with news about the runaway wheelchair. Mrs B had settled herself next to the window in the front seat, and Julie Mathison smiled at me when I took my place next to Barbara.

"Is your friend all right?" she called across the aisle.

"Yes," I replied, "Thank you for asking."

Mrs B looked straight ahead and ignored us.

Carol climbed onto the bus behind me and spoke to Mrs B. "Because of my size, it would be better if I sat where you and Julie are. Then I could stretch my legs out instead of being crunched up with my knees nearly touching my chest."

Mrs B glared at her. "Carol, I can't sit anywhere else. I get motion sickness when I can't see where I am going."

Carol sighed and continued down the bus to her seat.

"Why, hello, Mrs B," I said with – I hoped – a hint of cynicism. "Did you enjoy your day out?"

"If you must know, I didn't. I should have stayed at the Manor. It would have been much more pleasurable."

"Oh? What do you mean?"

She didn't answer, but turned away, signalling by body language she wanted no further conversation.

The driver started the bus. "Hang on. Don't take off yet," Barbara said, "I need to have a final check to ensure no one is left behind."

She rose from her seat and wandered up the aisle, counting heads. Satisfied everyone was on board; we set off for home.

On our way, we stopped again to take a toilet break at Campbell

Town. Barbara had refilled four thermoses of tea and coffee at the kiosk. However, there were no slices They had been eaten at lunchtime.

A weary crowd got off the bus where we arrived back at the Manor, but everyone, except Mrs B of course, agreed how much they had enjoyed the day. The bus driver, Barbara and Daisy, were thanked and given three cheers. After the bus was unloaded, willing hands grabbed the baskets and thermoses before everyone trundled up the steps into the Manor. The bus driver brought up the rear with the eskies. Everything from the bus was unloaded into the kitchen, where Daisy and Molly took charge of them.

"I'll be down later to check you properly," Barbara called to Judith as we walked towards our apartments.

As I made sure Judith was comfortable on her recliner, with a rug over her knees, there was a knock on the door.

Barbara poked her head around the door, "Can I come in?"

"Of course," Judith replied.

While I stayed to watch, Barbra gave her a thorough check-up, then smeared soothing lotion on her cuts and bruises.

After Barbara left, I asked Judith if she was feeling okay and perhaps she'd like to join me for tea in the dining room. Or would she prefer I brought a plate of sandwiches and a cake to her room.

"I'll be fine," she replied. "Don't fuss."

She still looked pale and tired as we walked to the dining room, and I decided to keep an eye out in case she became ill.

As we ate our tea of soup and sandwiches prepared by Molly, Judith perked up when some residents came across and commiserated with her about her mishap.

After tea, nobody dawdled. Worn out from their big day, almost the whole Manor was in bed and asleep earlier than usual. This included me, although dreams of Judith hurtling down the hill and into the pond kept me awake some of the time. Thoughts about who may have pushed Judith's wheelchair also preyed on my mind.

## Chapter 28

On the morning following the trip to the Botanical Gardens, Barbara and I sat in her office considering whether to pay a visit to Sergeant Plate and Constable McKellar

We discussed what had happened to Judith while we were at the gardens. My argument was if a push on the back of the wheelchair sent Judith careening down the hill could somebody, at the moment unknown, be attempting to kill the residents in the Manor. At this point, I hit a dead end. Why would anyone want to murder old people?

I turned to Barbara. "What do you say? Shall we visit Sergeant Plate at the police station? We can tell him about what happened to Judith and our suspicion that she had been pushed."

Barbara pursed her lips and shook her head. "No, I think the wise thing to do would be for us to bide our time. Make sure of our facts before we go barging in with speculations."

Persistence must be my second nature. "The Manor residents have been affected by the deaths and Judith's accident. If it was an accident."

Barbara tilted her head towards me and gave a brief weary smile. She stood up and looked over her desk at me and shook her head again. "No, Dimpy, we have no proof that anyone pushed Judith. We'll bide our time. The police seem to have closed their investigations for now. We need more proof that someone deliberately caused an accident to happen. By keeping our eyes open, I'm sure we'll learn more that way than by being busy-bodies annoying Sergeant Plate."

Oh well, persistence did not work this time, and she is the boss decision-maker at the Mountain View Residential Manor.

I meant to spend the afternoon working on my novel. By the number of emails that sat in my inbox, the publisher was not happy with the delay. My mind was too unsettled to concentrate on romantic entanglements. Instead, I took a walk around the park after lunch and tried to forget the worries at the Manor.

The sun sparkled on the water as I walked along the path near the river's edge. The grass, still damp from a recent shower of rain, glistened in the sunlight. With sensible forethought, I wore a light blue windcheater over my jumper, grey woollen slacks and practical laced up boots.

As I strolled, my thoughts turned to Judith's predicament. Her problems with her son, the signs of dementia and the trouble at the Botanical Gardens would have put a strain on her health. I resolved to do as everything possible to find a solution to her difficulties.

Out of the corner of my eye, I spotted movement in the river close to the bank. No ducks were around, so maybe it was a platypus. With cautious steps, heedless of the wet grass, I stood on the riverbank and peered into the water.

A deep growl came from behind me. I half turned around to see what was happening. Not in time, however, because a hard push into my back and legs almost made me stumble into the river. A twist as I fell caused me to land on my back. Above me, a dog as big as a small horse growled and stood with both paws on my chest. I remained still in case a sudden movement made it decide to bite.

"Sampson, come here, leave the woman alone," a voice demanded.

The dog eased off my chest and took off along the path. I lay without moving for a few minutes to catch my breath and make sure my arms and legs were under control. After a short time, I turned over onto my stomach, brought my knees towards my chest and pushed up into a sitting position.

A little farther down the path, I saw a man, with his back to me, put a lead on a huge mastiff. The dog glared in my direction and rumbled a low growl.

"Sorry about that," the man called out over his shoulder as he began to trot along the footpath, the dog loping beside him.

When I managed to stand up, there was a sensation of dampness on the back of my trousers from the wet grass.

An angry feeling coursed through me as I gazed at the marks on the riverbank where I had landed close to the water's edge. If I had not moved sideways, the force of the dog's paws would have sent me straight over the bank and into the river. A shudder went through me. The fast-flowing cold water could have caused me to drift under the bridge and into the rapids on the other side. Hypothermia or smashed on the rocks would not have been a nice way to die.

The dog and his thoughtless owner had disappeared as I limped over to a seat placed a few paces down from where I had landed.

Another niggle spread through me as I eased myself onto the bench. Most likely, I was wrong, but the quick glimpse of the dog's owner reminded me of Mrs B's son. If it were him, could he have deliberately set the dog on me and why? Another indignant consideration came to mind. Apart from the *sorry*, he seemed unconcerned about my wellbeing. There had been no attempt to see if the elderly lady was okay. He seemed more in a hurry to get away as fast as possible.

My heartbeat had begun to slow down to normal after the shock of the fall. Maybe my body would cope better after a hot shower and change of clothes. With slow steps, I left the park and crossed the road to the Manor.

Mrs B came down the corridor towards me as I reached my room. "What on earth happened to you, Dimpy? Did you have a fall?

"Yes, I did have –". I stopped speaking and gave her a thoughtful look. "I thought I saw your son in the park a little while ago. Does he own a dog?"

"Of course not. Gregory lives in a small one-bedroom flat in Launceston. He would not have room for a dog. Doesn't like them anyway." She pursed her lips, narrowed her eyes and gave me a suspicious look. "Why the sudden interest in my son?"

"No reason. A man I saw walking a dog by the river reminded me of him, that's all."

Mrs B sniffed and continued towards the rec room while I stepped into my apartment, slipped out of my clothes and into a lovely hot shower.

# Chapter 29

It was blowing a gale one evening four days after my near fall into the river. Outside my window, the rain sluiced down as lightning flashed and thunder rolled overhead. I dozed in front of the television, half-dreaming, half-listening to the evening news above the sound of wind and rain blown in from the Western Tiers.

A strange noise shook me out of my meditations.

At first, I assumed it was the television, then realised the sound came from the patio area. A knock against the glass window and a scratching sound like chalk on a blackboard. I swivelled my head in that direction, but the curtain over the glass doors blocked my view.

As I listened, there came another noise which sounded like someone groaning my name. My stomach lurched as my hand flew to the remote. I switched off the television, kept still and quiet and stared towards the patio door.

The sound came again, louder now. Someone or something was on my patio groaning and sobbing.

Without haste, I rose from my chair, crossed over to the glass door and switched on the outside light. Not knowing who or what to expect, I peeled the curtain back an inch or two and peered out. Through the rain and flashes of lightning, I could make out a dripping wet figure standing on the patio close to the entrance to my room.

"Dimpy, Dimpy, let me in," a voice trembled as I unlocked and opened the door. A wet, bedraggled figure stumbled into the room.

"Judith! Is that you?"

The figure nodded, teeth chattering and body shaking with cold. Judith's hair dripped, her clothes were soaked right through and made puddles on the carpet. Even her shoes seeped water.

"What on earth has happened?" No time to wait for a reply, Judith was not in a fit state to answer questions. Not yet, anyway. They would come later.

Although not sure of the symptoms for hypothermia, my first thought was to get her warm.

"You need a hot shower at once," I took Judith by the hand and led her across the living room to the ensuite door. "To thaw out before doing anything else. Your face has gone blue with the cold."

Opening the glass door, I turned the hot shower tap full force and added enough cold water from the other tap to bring the heat down to warm. "Okay, Judith, out of your wet clothes and into the shower while I find something for you to wear." Still worried about her, I added, "stay under the water until your body is nice and warm. Leave your clothes in a heap on the floor. We'll deal with them later."

As Judith undressed and climbed into the shower, I pulled clean towels from the cupboard and hung them on the rail in the ensuite.

"When you're ready to come out, dry yourself well. I've put my dressing gown over the towel rail and slippers near the bathroom door, so you can put them on after you dry yourself."

With a quick check to make sure she was wide awake and not

likely to fall onto the floor of the shower, I closed and locked the patio door, switched off the outside light, and closed the curtains.

About twenty minutes later, she emerged from the bathroom, looking more like her old self. She crossed over to a recliner, sat down and began to dry her hair with a towel. "Thank you, Dimpy. I don't think I've ever been so cold and miserable in my whole life as I felt stuck out there on your patio." As she spoke here had been a slight hesitancy in her voice.

"Stuck? How do you mean?"

"I'm not sure. One minute I was in my room, and the next I was standing in the grass at the bottom of my patio steps in the rain." She draped the towel around her neck and took a deep breath. "The outside light was not on, and the drawn curtains meant the patio windows and door to my room were in total darkness." Judith shook her head, and a sob came deep from her throat. "The night was so black, clouds covered the moon, and a cold wind was blowing while the rain beat down."

She took a deep breath, then continued to speak. "I stumbled up the steps onto the patio and fumbled my way to the door. I tried to open it, but the door was stuck or locked."

"Never mind, you're okay now," I said, in a comforting voice.

"Yes, Dimpy," Her voice became more robust. "As luck would have it, your light was on and shone through a crack in the curtains. I groped my way in your room's general direction, trying not to bump into too many things like shrubs and bushes. Hard going, I can tell you. Especially in the rain and wind." She rubbed the towel over her head. "I tripped over a couple of times in the dark. Anyway, the thing is I got here in the end – tired out, and shaking with the cold, which made it hard to knock on your door but still alive and kicking thank goodness. I'm so pleased you heard me."

So was I. Judith's already unstable condition, and her

tendency for memory loss now and then was bad enough. If you added the emotional trauma from her near miss on the runaway wheelchair at the Botanical Gardens, she was one lucky old lady.

"I'll put the kettle on," I said, and while it filled with water from the tap, I continued talking. "Once you're up to it, you can tell me what happened before you ended up outside in the dreadful weather."

A few minutes later, the kettle boiled, and tea made, we relaxed with a warm mug in our hands. I sat on the bed with my legs crossed, and Judith rested in the recliner.

"Earlier this evening, after dinner, Todd paid me an unexpected visit," she began. "I heard banging on the door, and when I opened it, there he stood smelling of beer and looking his usual scruffy self."

"Todd? As I recall, he treated you in an unkind way when he last visited," I said. "He harassed you over selling your house. I hope he still wasn't on about that this time. You were bad enough after his last visit. Upset for days following that experience." My voice had risen a notch; it was time to stop talking before I said too much. After all, Todd was her son, but Judith beat me to it.

"Yes, still nagging me about selling the house. He didn't even have the manners to ask how I'd been getting on, or about my health. He jumped straight in and ordered me to sell now. Said I was selfish. And when I stood up to him and told him I had no intention of selling, he turned nasty." She took a sip of her tea and stared at me, eyes wide and frightened. "He terrified me. His face became red and snarly looking, and he stared at me as if he wanted to …" her voice faltered. "To hurt me."

"Oh, dear, what a terrible way to act. Especially towards your mother." I now understood Judith's fear.

Judith sat back in the chair, took a couple of sips of tea to calm down and continued with her story. "He pulled a form from his pocket and waved it in my face and then pounded it with his fist. He said if I refused to sign it, the next time he came, he'd bring someone who'd make sure I did." She stopped talking and took another sip of tea. Her voice shook as she continued. "By this stage, he'd worked himself up into a terrible state. Globules of spit formed around his mouth and flew everywhere with every word he spoke. Then, after calling me a stupid, selfish old bitch, he told me I'd no choice. The house must be sold now like it or not." Another sip and a deep breath. "He stormed out of the room and slammed the door behind him."

Judith stood up and took her empty cup into the kitchenette. When she returned, she resumed speaking. "I am not sure what happened next. My mind was at sixes and sevens, and I couldn't think straight." With a puzzled expression, she continued, "I also have a suspicion Todd wasn't the only person who visited me tonight. Because of being so upset, with my mind in a whirl, it is difficult to remember. Nevertheless, something inside my head tells me someone else was there before I found myself outside in the rain."

"Think, Judith; this could be very important," I said, mulling over what had happened to Barry and Don.

Judith pursed her lips and wrinkled her bow. "I'm sorry, Dimpy, my mind's a blank. Maybe I imagined everything. I worry all the time about my memory problems. Could I have had a lapse and without meaning to ended up outside in the storm?"

Oh sure and managed to lock the patio door from the inside. But I kept that thought to myself.

"Come on; I'll walk with you to your room." I stood and placed my cup on the coffee table. "After a good night's sleep, you might remember about the other visitor."

While she used the ensuite in her apartment to change into her nightclothes, I looked around. There were a few things I wanted to check. I moved over to the door, which led to the

# Wendy Laing

patio and tried the handle. Yes, it was locked from the inside just as Judith had told me.

What I saw next left me in no doubt about a visitor. In the kitchenette, standing next to the sink, sat two used cups and saucers. I inspected the dregs in each cup and checked for lipstick on the rim. Todd, I was sure, would never drink tea. Besides, to imagine Todd sitting down with his mother to sip tea in a dainty china cup was laughable. It would never happen, even in the best of times.

I sat on the armchair next to Judith's bed, which looked cosy with three fat pillows and a plump, bright pink doona with large blue and yellow roses scattered all over. The television stood at the foot of the bed, and a bedside table held a Tiffany-style lamp, a small alarm clock and a television remote.

Who had been Judith's other visitor? The one she'd forgotten. And how on earth did she end up standing outside her apartment in the pouring rain?

When she emerged from the ensuite, she gave me back my gown and slippers, and I watched while she got into bed. "Thank you again, Dimpy. I think I'll be fine now."

"Okay but promise me you will make an appointment to see the doctor tomorrow and have a thorough check-up."

"Yes, I will. I promise."

I let myself out of her apartment and returned to mine. After picking up Judith's wet clothes from the bathroom floor, I put them into a plastic bag for washing the next morning. Her wet shoes could remain in the kitchenette. They would dry out on the patio in the morning if it stopped raining.

I made a small dram of whiskey with a splash of water and wished I could have a cigarette to go with the drink. However, I smothered the urge, took a sip and moved back into the lounge area.

As I relaxed in the recliner and put my glass on the coffee

table, thoughts came into my head about Judith's son. Something needed to be done about Todd. He was a nasty piece of work, and the stand over tactics being used to force his mother to sell the house had to be stopped as soon as possible. Nevertheless, I was sure in my mind that horrible as he was, he would not have pushed his mother out into the storm.

A possible solution to the Todd problem was forming in my mind. I resolved to see Judith's daughter at the earliest opportunity and tell her how Todd was behaving towards his mother.

## Chapter 30

Early Monday morning, after a shower and dressing in a tartan skirt and maroon twinset, I tidied the room.

The rain had stopped, and it looked like being a crisp, sunny day, ideal for what I had in mind – to get Judith sorted. I couldn't bear to see her putting up with Todd's nonsense any longer.

Judith's shoes were still damp, but the rain had stopped, so I put them on the patio to dry and took the bag, holding her wet clothes down to the laundry. After putting them in the washing machine, I went to the dining room for breakfast.

Later than usual and eager to see how Judith was faring, I barely nodded to Mrs B as I strode through the door. With a packet of cornflakes in one hand and a cup of tea in the other, I headed towards the table where Ronni and Judith were sitting, deep in conversation.

I nodded hello to them, as I placed my breakfast on the table. While I poured milk onto the cornflakes and buttered two slices of toast, Judith told me she had arranged an appointment to see the doctor at eleven o'clock that morning. "Great, Judith, you can tell us the results at lunchtime."

Ronni, who'd been sitting in silence while she finished eating her breakfast, pushed her empty plate aside and leaned forward, "Seeing a doctor? How come? You look fine to me, Judith."

"She is fine," I said. "However, she got wet through last night and needs a check-up. I'll explain it all to you later."

Judith and Dianne were having morning tea together at local café before the doctor's appointment. Then after she dropped her back at the Manor, Dianne would hurry off for a luncheon with some friends.

After we had eaten, and before Judith left, I explained that her wet clothes from last night were in the washing machine. I would hang them on the clothesline to dry, ready for her to pick up when she arrived back from the visit to the doctor.

"Okay. What's all the secrecy? What happened to Judith last night?" Ronni asked as we walked down the corridor.

"Have you time to have a coffee with me in my room? There's something else important to discuss with you. It's about Judith."

Once in my apartment, Ronni made herself comfortable on the recliner while I made mugs of coffee.

"Sorry to be mysterious," I said, handing her a cup and sitting down on the office chair. "You're wondering why she has gone to see the doctor. I'll explain, and then I want to ask your opinion about another matter. It might help with the situation she finds herself in with her son."

I told her about Judith being in a cold, wet and confused state on my patio last night and how Todd kept pressuring his mother to sell her house.

Ronni stared at me in dismay. "I had no idea this was happening. Please, if you can come up with a solution, I will do anything to help."

"It is a mystery her being out in the storm last night." I took a sip of coffee, and not concentrating, began to choke. Ronni patted my back as I wiped my mouth and eyes with a tissue. "As for Todd," I continued when able to speak again, "I intend to approach Judith's daughter, to ask if she would consider an

Enduring Power of Attorney. It may prove to be a way to stop Todd in his tracks." I took another careful sip of coffee. "What do you think of the idea?"

Ronni nodded. "Excellent, if it would make life easier for Judith, knowing Todd was not in a position to harass her anymore."

"However, I need a diversion. Could you waylay Judith when she returns from the doctor's visit and keep her out of the way while I have a word with her daughter before she leaves to visit her friends? If she sees me chatting to her daughter, she will want to know why."

"Of course, I can. Leave it to me. How long will you need?"

"About ten minutes should be enough. I must get through to Dianne how important this has become. Judith's health is at risk through worry about her son's continual nagging and bad behaviour. The fact Judith's memory is declining is a good excuse for something to be done as soon as possible."

Ronni looked at her watch. "It's after ten-thirty now, and by the time they have morning tea and see the doctor, it will be close to half-past eleven. Apart from drinking coffee, what are we going to do until they return to the Manor?"

We both sat in silent thought for a few minutes as we sipped.

"I have an idea," I said at last. "Perhaps we could do some gardening in the driveway and waylay them as they get out of Dianne's car."

"Great!" came the enthusiastic reply. "I'll return to my room and put on some gardening clothes and meet you at the front entrance in fifteen minutes."

Ronni in gardening clothes? This I had to see.

After she left, I raced into the laundry and hung Judith's washing on the clothesline to dry. The next thing to do when I returned to my room was to check Judith's shoes. Almost dry. Now, gardening clothes? In the wardrobe, there was an old pair of slacks and a jumper which had seen better days. I put them on and also changed my shoes for an old pair of runners. There were no rubber gloves, but perhaps Ronni had some tucked away in a drawer.

As arranged, we met at the entrance. Ronni's gardening clothes turned out to be dark blue slacks with a matching angora twin set. She carried a large, brimmed sunhat and wore a pair of brand new pure white gym shoes. Oh, yes, and she held two pairs of rubber gloves and a plastic garbage bag in the other hand.

"I nicked these from the kitchen," she told me.

"Didn't Molly or Daisy see you?"

"No, they were in the rec room having a coffee break."

We walked over to the middle of the driveway and stared at the garden. Barbara spotted us while we were still deciding what to do and came over to join us.

"What on earth are you two up to?"

"Gardening," I replied.

"Why? We employ a gardener to do this."

"We felt like some exercise," Ronni said.

She gazed at us in disbelief. "You look like a couple of refugees from the local gymnasium. Please be careful, you in particular, Dimpy. I don't want you tripping over a gardenia and landing in a rose bush."

"Of course, I won't do that, Barbara. By the way, where is the gardenia?"

Barbara shook her head, turned and walked back to her office. I could hear her stifling a giggle as she left.

"I don't think this will succeed, Ronni. We don't know the first thing about gardening. Working full time and then travelling when I retired before moving here kept me away from gardens. A nice little man cut the lawns and tidied everything for me."

"I also hired a gardener, Dimpy."

We sat on the lawn and stared again at the garden.

"I have a suggestion to make," said Ronni. "A walk in the park across the road would be preferable to standing in the garden like giant gnomes. If we take our time and chat, perhaps Judith will return soon."

"Good idea. Much better than trying to garden."

We left the rubber gloves on the steps at the entrance door, crossed the road to the park and meandered along the path. We took it in turn to keep a lookout for cars entering the Manor driveway. Ronni tucked her arm under my elbow as we walked. She is well aware of my ability to trip over if not watching where I put my feet.

While we strolled along, I told Ronni about being upended by a dog.

She laughed until tears appeared in her eyes. "It could only happen to you, Dimpy," she said, mopping her face with a handkerchief.

"Now, can you explain what an Enduring Power of Attorney is? I have never heard of it before," Ronni said as we sat on a seat with a clear view of the Manor entrance.

"Okay," I replied. "Briefly, it's a document that appoints somebody to sign and act on behalf of another person. It comes into effect when the person, for some reason, is ill or unable to manage his or her legal and financial affairs by themselves."

Ronni nodded. "Judith's mental abilities have deteriorated even more in the past few weeks, so she might allow her daughter to take one out."

"Dianne would be an excellent choice. I am sure she has her mum's best interest in mind and will be upset when we tell her about Todd's recent behaviour."

Ronni pointed across the road. "There they are now. We must get over there after Judith has gone into the Manor and intercept Dianne before she drives off."

We crossed the road at a fast pace and made it back to the Manor as Dianne kissed her mother and watched her walk into the reception area. She had not seen us hurrying across from the park.

Ronni followed Judith as I flagged Dianne down while she was reversing the car out of the driveway. I had no idea what Ronni would do or say to keep Judith occupied, but I expected that dressed as she was would be enough of a surprise. Especially the sun hat.

"Sorry to be a nuisance, Dianne," I gasped when she wound down her window and stared at me with surprise.

"I'm glad you caught me, Dimpy because I wanted to thank you for your quick action last night. Mum told the doctor all about it, and he examined her and said she was fine. Her lungs were clear, so she should not have after-effects such as pneumonia."

"That's great news because Ronni and I were worried. However, the reason I stopped you is because I needed to discuss Judith and your brother in private."

"Todd! What has he been up to now?"

When I told her how he had been harassing their mother to sell the house and borrowing money from her all the time, Dianne became upset.

"Mum doesn't need to sell the house, Dimpy. It's a bit of extra income for her."

I took a deep breath of relief. "I'm glad you agree, and I might have an answer that could stop this happening."

I explained about an Enduring Power of Attorney and told her she would find detailed information on the internet.

"It sounds like a perfect solution if I can persuade Mum to do it," she said. "I will check it over first and then talk to her about it. Above all, it is essential where Todd is concerned. Thanks, Dimpy." She rewound her window and drove out of the entrance, waving to me as she turned onto the street.

I found Judith and Ronni in the dining room.

"Judith has been telling me about the doctor's visit. I'll change for lunch now you're here," Ronni said and looked me up and down with a grin. "I think it might be a good idea if you did too."

As Ronni left, Judith laughed. "What on earth were you two doing out in the garden?" she said. "You know they have a gardener to do that."

"Yes, Barbara reminded us, so I guess we won't bother with the garden again. What did the doctor say?"

"He gave me a thorough check over and said I was fit as a fiddle in the body if not in mind. A funny thing to say I thought, but my memory does seem to desert me sometimes." Judith gave an anxious look. "I won't have to leave here will I, if my mind plays up?"

"Of course not, we'll make sure nothing happens to stop you living here." I hugged her. "Now I must change for dinner. See you soon."

Back in my room, I swapped my old clothes for a checked skirt and blue mohair jumper. Judith's shoes were dry, so I put them outside her apartment door. I felt pleased about the discussion with Dianne. She needed to take steps as soon as possible to stop Todd's harassment of their mother. I prayed it would work.

# Chapter 31

The next morning fluffy white clouds sat in wisps over the Great Western Tiers. There had been a storm during the night, but through the dining room window, I could see the rain had stopped, and the sun was shining.

Mrs B sat at her usual post inside the door, ticking off names. I gave her a brief nod and crossed over to the buffet table where I selected a light breakfast of cereal, toast with butter and jam, and a cup of tea.

Tray in my hands, I made my way to the table where Judith and Ronni sat tucking into their breakfasts.

"Are you doing anything interesting today, Dimpy?" Ronni asked as she poured milk over her cereal.

"Working on the novella this morning," I replied as I buttered my toast. "The emails from the publisher have begun to sound frantic."

"I look forward to reading your book when it is published," Judith said as she stood up and placed her breakfast plates and utensils on a tray. "I'm off to clean my room before the painting class begins. Bye, everyone."

"Copies of all your past books are in the bookcase in my lounge area. When your next novel is released, would you mind signing them all for me?" Ronni said as she also stood up, ready to leave. "A thorough clean and tidy up is on my list too. We can catch up for a chat at lunchtime." She carried her tray to the kitchen and followed Judith through the door and out into the corridor.

I finished my coffee, handed my tray of dirty dishes to Molly and walked back to my room.

On the computer, there was another ominous email from the publisher. For two hours, I wrestled with the heroine's attraction to the man with the perfect physique and the mind of a ten-year-old child. Unfortunately, because my mind kept returning to Judith's problems with Todd, I tended to write murderous phrases instead of romantic ones. I closed the laptop with a bang of frustration. There would be no sense trying to write a romantic novel while the deaths at the Manor still needed to be solved.

A visit to Sergeant Plate was a must-do, with or without Barbara's blessing. Time for someone to take the initiative. Although he had closed the cases, he needed a prod to keep investigating Don's and Barry's deaths. Maybe the people at the Manor could provide information about Barry and Don's actions in the days before they died. Anything was worth a try. After all, people were dying, not an unusual occurrence in an old folks' home, but not from overdoses and suicides. Did he, like me, suspect anything funny about these deaths, something not quite right?

Sergeant Plate also needed to know about Judith's accident at the Botanical Gardens and being locked out of her room in the storm. To me, both events seemed suspicious. Did a vicious murderer lurk in the Manor, attempting to kill or harm us all? We needed to know if this could be true. Would it be possible to find out who he or she was before more accidents or deaths occurred?

I needed to return my almost overdue library books. As the library was close to the police station, it gave me an excuse to call in and talk to Sergeant Plate on my way to replace them with new ones.

At the police station, I passed through the double glass doors into the customer service centre. Inside the entrance, a sudden thought came to me. Perhaps Sergeant Plate assumed I was a bit doddery, so made an instant decision to keep some distance between us and try not to fall over him again.

The four books were heavy, and it was a relief to stand them on the desk at the reception counter. I gave my name and asked the young constable if it would be possible to speak to Sergeant Plate on an urgent matter regarding the Mountain View Residential Manor.

He smiled and picked up the phone under the counter. "One moment, madam, and I will see if he is available."

I could see Sergeant Plate sitting at a desk near the wall through a glass window at the back of the counter. Deep in thought, he answered the phone on the corner of his desk. After a brief whispered conversation, he glanced over to where I stood, nodded and replaced the phone.

Sergeant Plate came to the door of his office area, held it open and beckoned me to enter. I picked up my books from the counter, stepped past him and walked over to his desk. The ex-librarian in me had fingers itching to tidy up the mess of files and folders spread from one end to the other. The sergeant brought over a chair from near the door. He placed it in front of his desk and indicated with a nod for me to sit down.

"How can I help you, er ... Dimpy?" he asked as he went around to the other side of the desk, took a seat, folded his arms across his body and stared at me.

Now, don't babble. I told myself, sitting down and placing my purse and books on the floor next to the chair.

"I know you don't consider the deaths at the Manor to be murder Sergeant Plate. However, a friend of mine, Judith

Milner, has recently had a couple of strange accidents where she could have ended up dead."

The sergeant blinked and sat straighter in his chair.

"As you know, some of the residents at the Manor, including me, still think Barry and Dons deaths were suspicious."

Sergeant Plate listened while I told him about Judith's claim her wheelchair had been pushed down the hill at the Botanical Gardens.

"Judith could have been killed if she hadn't landed in the duck pond. Lucky also that the wheelchair didn't topple onto her." As an afterthought, I added, "And the ducks managed to get out of the way."

The sergeant made some notes as I told him how Judith had found herself stuck out on the patio in the storm, unable to open the door to her room

"I checked the door when I took her back to her room and found it was locked from the inside." I took a moment to compose my thoughts. "If Judith had been out in that storm last night any longer there was a threat of pneumonia. She was close to hypothermia. At our age, this can become a death sentence."

Sergeant Plate sat forward in his chair and moved aside some of the files littering his desk, picked one up and opened it.

With a serious look in my direction, he said, "Thank you for telling me about your friend. I will make a note of everything you just told me in my file. It contains all the information we have made about events at the Manor since Barry Jackson's death. The manager at the Manor," he glanced at the file, "Barbara Wakefield told me how Mr Don Ahegge's death affected everyone. Especially yourself, Dimpy. I will, of course, let you know if anything arises from our talk today."

We both stood up, and I bent down to pick up my purse and library books. The sergeant came around to help me just as I lost my hold on the books. They landed with a heavy thud onto the sergeant's foot and spilled out across the floor. Sergeant Plate turned a funny shade of grey. He grimaced at me and shook his head, then bent and picked them up, and handed them to me along with my handbag.

Not sure whether to laugh or cry, I nodded my thanks

"It's all right, Dimpy, it didn't hurt me to have heavy books land on my shoe. At least, not too much, and I would prefer you to drop a few books rather than trip and knock me over."

The sergeant escorted an embarrassed old dame back through the reception area, passed the constable on duty, who was having a hard time trying not to laugh. He kept a firm hold on my arm – the one not holding the books – as we walked down the steps to the pavement.

"It has been a pleasure talking to you again, Dimpy," he said with a solemn look as he shook my hand. "I assume you are on your way to the library?"

"Yes."

"After you have changed your books, have a safe trip home. Oh, and please don't go tripping over anyone or anything on the way, will you?"

It occurred to me he had been holding on to make sure I didn't fall over anyone in the police station. Not that I would have had much of a chance, as he and the young officer at the desk were the only ones there. Constable McKellar must have been out on a case.

I thanked him for taking me seriously and hitched the bookbag higher onto my shoulder.

"Is there anything else I can help you with?"

"No, I'm fine."

Before crossing the road, I glanced behind and noticed him still watching me. So, I waved and received a wave in return.

At the library, I put my books one at a time through the return slot. While choosing new books from the shelves, I hoped Sergeant Plate *would* think seriously about what I had told him. Not dismiss my thoughts as ramblings of an elderly lady. My gut feeling told me there was something not right happening at the Manor. I worried in case there would be another death and hoped it would not be me.

There was a bus stop around the corner from the library, and it wasn't long before I reached home. From the book bag, I placed one book on the coffee table, and the rest on a shelf in the wardrobe. It was close to teatime, so after washing my hands and running a comb through my hair, I strolled to the dining room. With a plate of egg and lettuce sandwiches in one hand and a cup of tea in the other, I joined Ronni at a table where we sat for a while and discussed my visit with Sergeant Plate.

After watching Dimpy walk across the road to the library, Sergeant Plate strode back into the police station, his lips pursed in thought, and stopped at the reception counter.

"When she returns, will you please ask Constable McKellar to see me," he instructed the man on duty there.

"Will do, sir," was the reply.

Dimpy might be old, he thought as he walked over to his desk, but she still has a sharp eye and mind. I shouldn't discount her worries about unusual occurrences at the Manor.

He rummaged through the files on his desk, found the one he wanted and wrote some notes about the accidents before putting it to one side. He sat back and thought about everything Dimpy had said transpired over the past weeks concerning her friend and resolved to discuss the details with Constable McKellar. Perhaps they might even pay a visit to the Manor and talk to the manager again. Two heads would be better than one, he thought, but the idea of somebody or somebodies attempting to kill the residents did not gel. What was there to gain by killing off the old people who lived there?

## Chapter 32

The next morning, I finished the final draft of my novel and emailed the attachment to the publisher. There was time to visit Barbara with the news about Judith's latest mishap and my visit to the police station before lunch. I knocked on Barbara's door, poked my head into the office and asked to speak to her. Seated opposite me, she listened as I described how Judith had been locked out of her unit during a storm a few nights ago.

"The police need to know about this," she said, "as soon as possible."

"I have already done that."

"You have?"

"Yesterday I visited the police station and told Sergeant Plate about what had happened to Judith at the Botanical Gardens and on my patio last night," I replied. "And there is something else you need to know. It concerns her son, Todd."

Barbara was shocked to hear the news Judith's son had been harassing her for money and attempting to force her to sell her house.

"I've spoken to her daughter, Dianne, about invoking an Enduring Power of Attorney to put an end the persistent pestering and nastiness," I said. "Dianne liked the idea and will discuss it with her mother as soon as possible."

"If it will be of assistance, it's an excellent plan. Please let me know the outcome and if there is anything I can do to help."

Our conversation came to a halt when we heard running feet in the reception area. The office door flew open and crashed into the wall. The sudden draught and the resounding crack caused us both to turn and stare.

Ronni staggered through the doorway. She puffed and panted as she collapsed onto the floor.

"Help, I think I've been poisoned." Ronni's voice shook with fear as she hoisted what appeared to be a small jar of coffee above her head.

Without wasting any time, I raced over to Ronni and knelt next to her. Her face, colourless as cream and covered in the oily sticky sweat, was a dead giveaway. Something terrible was happening to her.

With Barbara's assistance, I half lifted, half pulled her from the floor and guided Ronni to the nearest seat, the one I had been using. She collapsed like a cloth doll, head lolling towards the ground. Her shoulders heaved as she attempted to take deep breaths. I heard Barbara's voice ordering an ambulance.

One at a time, I removed her fingers from around the jar and placed it on the desk.

It was obvious to see she was getting worse. Her body started to twitch, and her eyes, stretched and frantic, were screaming her pain.

"Dimpy fetch a blanket and a couple of pillows from the bed in the next room, would you," Barbara ordered. "We have an extremely sick lady on our hands. The ambulance will be here in about ten minutes," She turned Ronni's hand over and felt for a pulse. "We can't do anything else for her now except keep her calm and make sure she is as comfortable as possible."

This stirred me into action. I hurried into the bedroom and pulled a blanket, and two pillows into my arms then staggered back to the office. After arranging the pillows and covering Ronni with the blanket, we sat on the edge of our seats. With our eyes trained on Ronni, we waited for the ambulance to arrive.

My hand shook as I rummaged through my pockets, found some clean tissues, and wiped the sweat from Ronni's brow. I adjusted the blanket, held her hand and in as familiar a voice as possible told her not to worry, the ambulance was on its way.

By now I'd became extra worried. With a sudden movement, Ronni started to moan and arch her back. What is taking the ambulance so long, I wondered casting a frantic glance towards the front entrance, which was easy to see through the open office door. They should be here by now. I checked my watch. Only five minutes had passed since Barbara called them.

Another look at Ronni showed how restless and in pain she was. Her head moved from side to side on the pillows. Underneath the blanket, her legs moved up and down with a jerky movement. With face ashen, lips pale and slack, her breaths became more shallow and uneven.

Unable to stay seated, Barbara paced up and down between the door and where Ronni sat.

"She's ... getting worse," I said with an anxious look in Barbara's direction. Sobs caught in my throat made it difficult to get the words out.

Barbara wrapped an arm around my shoulders. "She will survive. Ronni is a fighter," I hoped she was right.

We both turned our heads toward the door and with sighs of relief, heard the sound of a siren coming towards us. A few minutes later, the ambulance, lights flashing, drew up outside the entrance to the Manor. Two paramedics, a male and a female in their blue and white uniforms, hopped out as I ran up to them.

"You'll need to hurry," I said, my voice screeching with worry. "We think she's dying."

They ran to the back of the ambulance and opened the double doors. Then grabbed their equipment and followed me to where Barbara knelt next to Ronni. In a calm voice, she was telling Ronni to hang in there; the ambulance had arrived.

Remembering what a nuisance I had been to everyone in Don's room, almost knocking a paramedic over and landing on the patient, it was time for me to stand out of the way. There appeared to be nothing more I could do. Ronni was in good hands. I stood near the desk in the reception area and hoped and prayed Ronni would survive.

One of the paramedics raced past me and out to the ambulance. She pulled out the stretcher and hurried back with it to the office.

Only about five minutes ticked by before the paramedics passed me again, this time heading for the ambulance with Ronni, covered by a sheet, lying on the stretcher. I heaved a sigh of relief to see that the sheet did not cover her head.

"How is she?" I called as they made their way out the front door. A grim answer came that she was stabilised and should make it to the hospital for an assessment by a doctor.

After the ambulance left, lights blinking and siren at full blast, I stood with Barbara on the front steps of the Manor and watched it disappear towards the hospital.

Other residents had gathered in the reception area. They talked in low voices as they watched the ambulance disappear up the road.

With a defiant expression, Barbara said, "There is nothing more we can do now, Dimpy. It is up to the doctors to keep her alive."

Julie Mathison detached herself from the group of watchers and asked, "What has happened to Ronni?"

"She may have been poisoned," Barbara replied. "Please return to what you were doing, and I will let you know when we receive word from the hospital about Ronni's condition." She turned to me. "Ronni *is* a fighter, Dimpy, and she will find a way to get through this."

There was a sob in my voice as I answered. "I hope so, Barbara."

Barbara put an arm around me, and we walked back into her office. Once there she collapsed into a chair. "I'll ring the hospital in a few hours, and perhaps we will have news, GOOD news, Dimpy," she said with a stern expression in my direction.

The jar had stood, forgotten, next to where Barbara was sitting. I picked it up and stared at it. When we moved into the Manor, the kitchen staff gave all the residents a similar, small glass jar with a screw-top lid full of coffee to keep in our apartments. A similar type of glass jar contained our tea bags. When empty, we took them back to the kitchen and received a refill.

With Barbara beside me, I peered through the glass at the grains of coffee. Now and then when shaken, dark, metallic specks appeared, quite a few in fact.

"I am going to ring the police," a grim-faced Barbara said. "This jar needs to be checked. There is a foreign substance mixed in with the coffee. It will need analysing as soon as possible, and those grains identified."

"Yes, and urgently, because it could help the hospital decide what type of poison they are dealing with," I replied.

Barbara nodded and replaced the jar on the desk.

"I'll go back to my apartment now and wait there," I said as Barbara searched through a drawer for a plastic bag. "Please ring me the minute you have any news?"

"Of course," Barbara replied, busy placing the jar into a plastic bag.

Before leaving, I collected the blanket and pillows from the floor where the paramedics had thrown them and put them back in the bedroom while Barbara phoned the police station.

In my room, miserable, worried, and afraid Ronni would not survive, I lay on the bed and sobbed. To lose another friend in such a cruel way would be heart-breaking. However, Ronni would not be happy with me giving in to gloom and doom like this. *Dry your eyes, pull yourself together and check your emails, there may be something among them to keep you occupied.*

The booted-up computer proved to be an inspiration, for a little while at least. There was an email from the publisher accepting my latest draft manuscript. He had attached two covers for me to choose from, plus a small list of edits that needed minor changes. I gazed at the book covers and checked the amendments, but somehow the thrill of having my novel published was missing. Concentration on alterations and decisions about a front cover was difficult while worrying my friend could be dying.

So, I had been right all along; the recent deaths in the Manor had not been natural or accidental. Someone was attempting to murder the residents one by one. And I had no idea who—or why.

# Chapter 33

In my heart, I didn't feel up to it, not one little bit, but it had to be done. Explain to Judith, our friend Ronni had been poisoned. As vague and doddery as Judith had become nowadays, she needed to know. I felt sure she would never forgive me if the news were kept from her, or she found out from someone else in the Manor.

Face washed, and fresh makeup applied I knocked on her door. There was no answer, but Mrs B banged her way past me and stopped to say Judith and her daughter were in the rec room.

For a brief moment, I deliberated on whether Mrs B made a habit of loitering in the passageway all day. I seemed to run into her there a lot. Did she know about Ronni? I shook my head. No, she would have grilled me for details if she had known.

When I arrived at the rec room, I found Judith and Dianne sitting at the windows sipping coffee and gazing out at the view of the Western Tiers. Although it was spring, snow-caps were hugging the highest peaks and shone in the sunlight. I grabbed a coffee and went over to join them.

"No!" Judith cried when I told her the news about Ronni. "I can't believe it. She ate breakfast with us this morning, and everything seemed normal then. Didn't it?" Her lips quivered, and eyes welled up with tears.

Instead of replying, I nodded because I also found it hard to speak.

Dianne came to the rescue. "It's okay, Mum." She hugged Judith and handed her a tissue from her purse. "Ronni is one of your best friends; it's okay to be upset about what has happened to her."

"Thanks, Dianne," Judith said, dabbing her eyes with the tissue. She seemed to have recovered, although she'd lost a lot of colour in her face. "It's tough to believe. As I remember it, Ronni left the dining room shortly after you this morning, Dimpy."

Judith's face wasn't gaining any colour. Tears still filled her eyes, and her hands began to shake. I couldn't take my eyes from her, worried she might faint with the shock.

"Why don't you rest on your bed for a while," I suggested. "Dianne and I will have a little chat. Then we'll pop in to make sure you are all right. We won't be long … only a few minutes. Okay?"

Judith didn't argue. She pushed her chair back, rose to her feet and after the slightest of nods to each of us, left the room, her steps slow and a little unsteady.

"Will Mum be okay?" Dianne asked with an anxious glance towards Judith.

"I hope so. But just in case I will not hold you up for long."

I fetched another coffee for each of us from the urn and asked if she had found time to think about the Enduring Power of Attorney.

"I haven't had time to look up the Attorney business on the internet. Can you explain in a little more detail about what it entails?" Dianne took a sip of coffee and replaced her cup in its saucer. "How does it work again?"

"It's simple," I said. "It's a document prepared by a solicitor. Somebody – usually a close relative – is given the authority to sign and act on behalf of another family member who may be having problems coping with everyday matters. The solicitor would assist with the legal details regarding your ability to make decisions about your mother's future. They would arrange for the necessary papers to be signed, giving you the Enduring Power of Attorney over your mothers' affairs."

"Including decisions about her house?"

"Yes".

Dianne chewed her bottom lip as she thought about what I had said. "Where does Todd come into all this?" she asked.

"He won't; once accomplished, he doesn't have a say. If Judith is agreeable, you would have the final ruling over all matters concerning your mother."

Dianne became quiet, thinking again. "Crikey," she said. "It's a lot to take in."

Mission accomplished, I suggested we look in on Judith. If her mother were calm enough, Dianne could ask for her opinion about an Enduring Power of Attorney idea as a way to stop Todd's harassment.

We found Judith sitting in her recliner. Colour had returned to her face, which still had a drawn and tired look. Dianne explained the basics to her. I made it clear that they needed a solicitor to discuss all the details before making any decisions.

Judith liked the idea and wanted to put it into place right away. Dianne phoned a solicitor in Launceston and made an appointment for the following day. I figured it was time to leave. Mother and daughter had a lot to talk over.

Before I left, Judith asked if she could visit Ronni in the hospital. I assured her she would be the first to know after Barbara gave me the details about Ronni's condition.

With this in mind, I headed for Barbara's office to enquire whether the hospital had contacted her yet.

I knocked, entered and found Sergeant Plate and Constable McKellar in the room, talking to Barbara.

"Ah, Dimpy, the constable and I were about to send out a search party for you," he said. "I called in to let you know your friend, Ronni is out of danger. She's still in intensive care, but a nurse told us her condition is stable."

"What happened to her?" I asked. "Was it poison?"

"Yes. The substance was mixed with the coffee in the jar Mrs Wakefield gave me earlier today. The extreme nature of her back spasms – a sure sign – told the doctors strychnine could be the type of poison administered. That's all we know at the moment, but tests are in the process of being done as we speak."

"Is she allowed to have visitors yet?"

Barbara shook her head. "Not at the moment because she's still in intensive care. When they move her to a ward, you can visit her."

As I was about to leave, the sergeant stopped me. "Before you go, call in and see me at the police station sometime, would you? I'd like you to give Constable McKellar a statement about Mrs Goodman's movements yesterday. There are some things I may want to ask you. Pick your brain, so to speak, about the background of the residents living in the Manor."

After a nod to let him know I'd heard what he said, I made my way back to my room. The last few days had been exhausting. My heart began to beat so fast; I thought I would pass out. *Deep breaths, Dimpy, breathe in and hold, then a gradual release out again.* After ten deep breaths, my heart rate came down to normal. If this kept up, the murderer would be the least of my worries; I'd most likely die of a heart attack instead.

With luck, Ronni would be able to receive visitors soon. I needed to see for myself that she would be okay. With that in mind, I returned to the office and asked Barbara to open the door to Ronni's apartment with the master key. In the wardrobe, I found a small travel case large enough to hold a dressing gown and two negligees, a change of clothes and underwear, make-up and a hairbrush. Ronni would hate to have people visiting her while not looking at her best.

My next visit was to Judith not only to give her an update about Ronni but also to check she was okay.

When I entered the dining room at teatime, people came over to where I sat gazing at an uneaten sandwich. They wanted news about Ronni, and I told them all I knew. Ronni had been poisoned and was slowly recovering in the hospital. I'd lost my appetite, so I returned my sandwich to the kitchen and walked back to my apartment.

A stiff whiskey was more to my liking. I decided to have two, then watched an old movie before going to bed. Nothing worked. Instead of a good night's sleep, I tossed and turned. Visions of not only Ronni but Barry and Don crowded into my mind. In the end, utter exhaustion caught up, and I dropped into a restless slumber.

## Chapter 34

Two mornings later, still worried about Ronni, I rang the hospital, and the receptionist said Ronni was out of intensive care and well enough to have visitors. Straight away, I ordered a taxi to take me to the hospital.

Now Ronni appeared to be out of danger; the doctor had her moved to a single room on the second floor. She was so pleased to see me. I, on the other hand, was shocked to see her. Being a naturally thin person, in the space of a few days, she seemed to have become old and frail. She perked up when I gave her the case. "Thank you, Dimpy, always so thoughtful. Be a dear and pull the curtain across so I can change into a clean nightie, put on a touch of makeup and style my hair."

When the curtain opened once more; a happier, normal-looking Ronni made her appearance.

Perched on the bottom edge of the bed, I realised it was time to find out how she thought the strychnine could have been placed into the jar.

"The police have already taken a statement from me. I can only tell you what happened when I arranged to have my coffee jar refilled."

She made herself comfortable in the bed; the sheet tucked around her body with two pillows behind her head. "I took my jar up to the kitchen and asked Molly if she would fill it with coffee for me while I collected my washing from the dryer in the laundry. When I returned, the full container was sitting on the buffet table in front of the kitchen door. I took both the jar and my laundry back to my room."

"Did you see anyone hanging around near the dining room?"

Ronni thought for a moment, her eyes shut in concentration. "Mrs B passed by in the corridor while I handed the jar to Molly, but I didn't take much notice as my laundry basket was heavy, and I was in a hurry to do my washing."

"Was she or anyone else around when you picked up the full jar of coffee from the kitchen?"

Again, Ronni sat in silence for a few minutes in thought before shaking her head. "No one was in the dining room or kitchen, not even Molly."

"What made you think the coffee was poisoned?"

"I realised there was something wrong after taking a few sips. There was a sour, metallic taste in my mouth."

I left the hospital more relieved than when I had arrived knowing this plucky old bird would make a complete recovery.

As soon as I returned to the Manor, I needed to find Molly. She may have seen someone loitering around the dining room while Ronni's jar sat unattended on the bench. However, there was no-one in the kitchen or dining room. Maybe I could catch up with her at lunchtime.

I called into Judith's apartment and told her Ronni was allowed to have visitors. She rang the hospital while I was there and arranged a visit for later that morning. Judith hoped to be back in time to join me for lunch. My appetite had returned after seeing Ronni in the hospital and knowing she would recover.

Once more feeling energetic, I vacuumed the unit, cleaned the ensuite and changed the sheets. This filled in time until noon. In the ensuite, I brushed my hair, added a touch of lipstick, then locked the door behind me and walked to the dining room.

As I helped myself to the casseroles and sweets, Molly came out from the kitchen with another hot dish to place on the table. My chance, at last, to ask her about Ronni's coffee jar.

She told me as far as she could remember, no one except Ronni came into the dining room when she dropped off the jar. After Ronni had left, she spent about twenty minutes cleaning the kitchen area before filling the jar with coffee. She left it on the bench for Ronni to pick up and had gone to the shops to buy a packet of nutmeg to sprinkle on the custard for tomorrows pudding. When Molly returned to the kitchen a few hours later, the jar was gone. She assumed Ronni had taken it back to her room.

As I walked to one of the spare tables, Carol and Julie Mathison beckoned me over to where they were sitting. "We noticed you were by yourself," Carol said, "so come and join us. It's not much fun eating lunch alone, and besides, we hoped you had an update on Ronni."

"Thank you," I said while unloading my tray of food onto the table. "The good news is that she is out of intensive care and moved into a single room on the second floor. However, I don't know when she will be allowed to return to the Manor."

"Judith not lunching today?" Julie asked.

"She's gone to visit Ronni. I'm not sure if she will be back in time for lunch."

"Barbara has arranged for a group of musicians to entertain us. They'll be here at two o'clock this afternoon," Carol said. "You are welcome to join us. It will last for about an hour and a half."

"They play Dixieland jazz," chimed in Julie.

"Yes, thank you. That would be great," I replied. Maybe it would take my mind to a better place than it was at the moment.

The casserole had been delicious, and I had begun to eat my jellied fruit and cream when Judith came into the dining room and made a beeline for us. She nodded to Carol and Julie as they stood up and gathered their plates and cutlery.

"We'll leave you now Judith's here to keep you company," Julie said. "We're going to Carol's apartment for a coffee. We'll meet you in the rec room later."

"Okay," I said.

The ladies waved as they disappeared out the door.

When Judith came back with her food, she spoke between mouthfuls. "Dianne met me at the solicitor's yesterday afternoon. The meeting gave us a lot to think about." She stopped talking for a moment to eat more casserole. "Mm, this is nice. Now, where was I? Oh yes. Once the Power of Attorney was explained to us, I was happy for her to take over handling the details of the house and help me with my finances." She finished her casserole, put it to one side then dipped her spoon into the jellied fruit and cream. "We signed the agreement and thank you for thinking of such a great idea. The next time Todd comes to visit and starts harassing me about the house, I will let him know what I have done." She sighed and put down her spoon. "Todd won't be happy, but Dianne said to send him to her to deal with if he turned nasty."

As we walked back to our apartments together, I told Judith there would be a jazz group in the rec room that afternoon.

"What time, Dimpy?"

"Carol told me it starts at two o'clock."

Judith said she would join us for the concert, although she wasn't a big jazz fan.

Back in my room, I decided to read one of the four library books that had accumulated on the table next to the bed. It was time to put all thoughts of the attempted murder into the back of my mind. At least for a little while.

# Chapter 35

At the concert, I sat next to Carol, Julie and Mrs B. "Why hello, Emily, I wasn't aware you were a jazz fan?"

"I'm not, but it is something to do in this boring place."

Judith still had not joined us when the band started playing, so I put my bag on the empty seat next to me to keep it free for her.

The band – a quartet of bass, sax, piano and drums began to play a breezy rendition of *When the Saints Go Marching In*.

They were well underway and judging by the handclapping and foot-tapping were being enjoyed by the audience when *Swing Low, Sweet Chariot* came to an abrupt halt.

The door to the rec room flew open with a bang that almost took it off its hinges. Todd, followed by his mother, who was trying to hold him back, burst into the room. All heads turned in their direction.

"Let me go, you bloody old bat," he yelled, trying to shake off his mother who held on to his sleeve in a firm grip. "I have something to say to her!" His index finger was pointing straight at me.

He managed to shake off his mother's hand and pushed her out of his way. Then he strode into the room oblivious to the crowd who had been listening to the music. All four band members stood still holding their instruments. They stared around in astonishment, wondering what was going on.

Judging by the wild look on Todd's face as he pushed himself through the seats towards me, I was about to find out.

Todd tossed the chair next to me out of his road. He loomed at my side with his hands clenched and scowled. "You're nothing but a bloody troublemaker," he said, shouting and spitting in my face. "I know what you've been up to, Dimpy—putting bloody ideas into my mother's head. What's this about a bloody Power of Attorney you interfering old biddy?" Spittle dripped down his chin; he wiped it away with a sudden thrust of his hand. "Mrs B, or whatever you call her, waylaid me on my way to my mother's room after lunch and told me all about this thing you talked my mother into taking out."

I gazed at him, fascinated by the way his face appeared to draw in on itself as he fought for breath. His face had also turned a nasty red colour. Despite smelling the pungent odour of beer on his breath and not sure how much Dutch courage that might give him, I decided to take my chances.

I stood straight up to all of my six-foot-two height and glared at him. "Listen, you nasty little worm," I said, looking down to the top of his head. "You've been treating your mother like a piece of dirt. She's terrified of you." By this time, I was giving him a piece of my mind at the top of my voice. "And if your mother decided to take out an Enduring Power of Attorney to stop your nastiness then good on her. If it means you can't force your mother to sell her home, then I am pleased I interfered." Taking a deep breath, I continued, "Go and talk to your sister, if you have the guts, and she'll tell you all about it."

"I'll get you for this," he said, jabbing a finger into my chest. "You just bloody wait and see." Then, as though noticing for the first time everyone was staring at him, he lowered his finger, turned on the spot and strode as far as the door. In his anger, and not watching where he was going, he almost tripped over an upturned chair. With a kick of his foot, the chair skittered along the floor. He turned to face everyone. "You're a mob of interfering bitchy old crones," he spat. "I'll get even with you for this." Then, giving a two-finger salute, he strode through the door into the corridor.

We heard the door at the main entrance slam shut as he left the Manor.

Shaking my head, I restored the overturned chair to its normal position. "It's okay; he's gone," I said in general to everyone.

There came a low buzz as the audience settled back into their seats, and the jazz band began playing again.

Judith still stood next to the doorway, lost for words. I walked over to her, and she collapsed into my arms, sobbing quietly, ashamed of her son's behaviour.

"It will be okay, Judith. I'll let Dianne know what happened. When she and her husband get through telling him off, Todd might leave you alone for a long time."

Judith gave a watery giggle. "Actually," she said," I like the phrase 'bitchy old crones'. Maybe we should have tee-shirts made up with it written across the front."

"Great idea," I said. "Now let's go back to my place and have a nice cup of tea."

"Yes; I'd like that. Although perhaps something stronger for me."

A picture of my whiskey bottle drifted through my head. I nodded.

"Me too".

# Chapter 36

As we drank our tea, Judith gave me her daughter's phone number. After she left, I used my mobile to telephone Dianne and explained how Todd had behaved towards his mother and me at the jazz concert. She sounded distraught at the news.

"Damn and blast Todd. I will be there soon to make sure Mum is okay. Todd's going to cop a good talking to when I catch up with him."

However, something kept needling me. An uneasy sensation had crept in regarding the suspicions going through my mind about Mrs B. She always seemed to be in the vicinity when something nasty happened. Lurked in the corridor and watched through beady eyes when first Barry then Don died. Her son worked at a pharmacy and had access to medication and poisonous substances. Although she would find it difficult to climb up the hill at the Botanical Gardens and push Judith's wheelchair, it was not an impossibility. If the son were in cahoots with his mother, it could have been him using a dog to try to drown me in the river.

Was Mrs B Judith's unknown visitor the night of the storm? Had the tea she drank before she found herself out in the rain been tampered with and drugged? Perhaps with some kind of tranquiliser. Mrs B would find a pliable Judith easy to manipulate through the patio door before locking it.

When the poison was put into the jar of coffee, Ronni was busy in the laundry, and according to Molly, no one had entered the dining room. However, she had gone shopping and left the jar of coffee in the dining room for Ronni to pick up. It would have been easy to Mrs B to poison the coffee without being seen.

The flaw to most of this was Mrs B's cane. Because as soon as she left her room, you heard it loud and clear. Besides, being a nasty, bad-tempered old lady didn't make her a murderer.

The suspicion Mrs B was involved in everything that had happened lately would not go away. I needed to speak to Sergeant Plate. Maybe this time, he would listen to my theory without rejecting the idea. I headed for Barbara's office to ask if she would come to the police station with me. Her door was open, and I was pleased to see Sergeant Plate seated in front of her desk.

As I walked into the office, I spotted Mrs B sitting in a chair near the window. She sat upright; her usual scowl in place and the cane held between her legs with both hands.

"Dimpy!" Sergeant Plate exclaimed. "We were about to put out a call for you. Mrs B has an interesting story to tell."

"Hello, Sergeant Plate," I said, nodding to Barbara and Mrs B. I spotted Constable McKellar sitting in a far corner of the room nearly hidden by a pot plant. Everyone was seated—except me, but I was content to stand. What I had to say would be better expressed in an upright position. "I'm glad to find you here, sergeant, I wanted to discuss the deaths and accidents that have been happening at the Manor."

I was about to speak my piece when the sergeant beat me to it. "So, Dimpy, that was quite a skirmish back there at the jazz concert. Mrs B told us you were right in the middle of it."

For a moment, I was confused, then I understood; this was a set up by Mrs B to made me look bad in the eyes of Sergeant Plate and Barbara.

"Yes," I said. "I was in the middle of it. That's because I care about Judith. She has been subjected to constant harassment by her obnoxious son, Todd. He wanted only one thing from his mother – the money from the sale of her house. He's not concerned about how feeble or confused his mother has become. He only wants to get his hands onto Judith's money so he can feed his drinking habit ... drugs too, I suspect." All eyes watched me as I continued to speak. "Judith's daughter needed to know about Todd's behaviour towards his mother and me, so I rang her. Together she and I had suggested an Enduring Power of Attorney idea to Judith."

Sergeant Plate frowned as though puzzled. "All very well, Dimpy but there's something you're leaving out; you weren't coming here only to tell us about the quarrel, were you? You wouldn't come here only to tell us about a fight." He turned to face the constable. "Did you also get that impression, Constable McKellar?"

As though surprised by the sudden intrusion on her thoughts, the constable's head popped up with a start. "Um ... yes, sir," she said, with an awkward wriggle, "I got that impression."

Sergeant Plate turned his gaze towards me. "According to Mrs ... er ... B, you always seemed to be in the area when the deaths of Barry Jackson and Don Ahegge occurred? At the Botanical Gardens, you were the person who talked Judith into sitting in a wheelchair at the top of the hill."

Constable McKellar looked up from her notepad. "And supposedly 'rescued' Mrs Milner from the patio when she was outside in the storm," she said.

Mrs B perched in her chair staring at me, a self-satisfied smirk on her face. A light bulb lit up in my head. Oh, no, surely they didn't think I had anything to do with the deaths or accidents. Had Mrs B sensed I knew she was behind everything that had happened and set out to blame me? Blow it, I came here to tell

Barbara and Sergeant Plate what I knew – or thought I knew – so that's what I'd do, despite the consequences if I was wrong. I took a deep breath and began to speak again.

"You're right; I do have something else to say." I swivelled my head till my eyes locked onto those of Mrs B. "It's obvious Mrs B is attempting to blame me for the awful things that have been happening, which is a lie. Why would I try to hurt my friends? All I hoped to do was solve the mystery surrounding their deaths and accidents." A sob came from my throat. Determined not to cry, I pointed towards Mrs B. "This woman provoked Judith's son, Todd, into confronting me at the concert. She told him I advised Judith to see a solicitor about an Enduring Power of Attorney." I turned back to face Barbara. "She hoped there'd be a scene, which you would have to deal with straight away. That wouldn't go down very well with the Board of Management; it could even lead to my being asked to leave the Manor."

Barbara, who'd kept quiet during all this, now spoke up. "Oh, I think you're exaggerating a trifle there, Dimpy. Anyway, why on earth would Mrs B want to do that?"

I noticed Mrs B's hands tighten around the top of her stick as she leaned forward and the shake in her voice was noticeable when she spoke. "Yes, Dimpy, why on earth would I want to do that?"

"Perhaps for the same reason you killed Barry and Don and tried to kill Judith and Ronni."

Sergeant Plate and Constable McKellar sat up straight on their seats and stared at me.

"Wh—what are you saying?" the sergeant said. "Mrs B is the murderer?" Then, thinking like any good policeman, he asked, "Do you have proof of your somewhat wild accusations? Solid proof?"

"I know Dimpy well," Barbara said in her best managerial

voice. "She wouldn't say things like this if there weren't any substance to them, so I'd listen if I were you."

"Thanks, Barbara," I said, gaining the courage to go on after her kind words. "I believe Mrs B has been desperate to move into a patio apartment which, I have to admit, are more desirable than the single units elsewhere."

An interruption came from Mrs B. "What Dimpy – Margaret Gruar – has told you is correct. I've always been a lady of means, not used to living in squalor, which I'm subjected to here. Reduced to living in a tiny bed-sitter ... how demeaning. I deserved much better."

"That is why she poisoned Barry and Don and tried to kill Judith and Ronni," I said, turning to face her.

"What a load of rubbish, Dimpy. I dare you to prove those insinuations against my good name."

A thought must have flashed somewhere in Barbara's brain. "The lists of names you ticked before breakfast every morning." She turned to Mrs B. "You weren't helping the staff; you were checking to see who had or had not survived the night in case any patio apartments became vacant."

Sergeant Plate gave an exasperated sigh. "Have you anything else to say, Mrs ..." He looked back at Barbara over his shoulder. "For pity's sake, what is this woman's proper name?"

Mrs B rose from her seat. "It's Mrs Emily Barraclough. And if you are through with your stupid suspicions about me, I am leaving."

All was quiet as we listened to Mrs B's cane slamming down the corridor. Sergeant Plate broke the silence. He had heard enough. "You're right Dimpy; we have no proof, only your word Emily Barraclough is a murderer. A patio is no excuse for killing people."

He held up his hand to stop me interrupting. "Although, after hearing you speak just now, I am inclined to think you are innocent of everything, except knocking me over now and then." He turned to Barbara and said, "Constable McKellar and I will return to the police station and discuss the information we have received this afternoon. We will talk to you again soon. Coming, Constable?"

"Yes, sir."

"Goodbye, for now, ladies," he said as they left the room.

We could hear them in muted conversation as they walked toward the main entrance.

I glanced at Barbara. "What on earth was that all about anyway? How could anyone believe I would kill or hurt my friends? All I want to do is find a solution and sooner rather than later."

As Barbara opened her mouth to reply, I continued. "I know Mrs B is the culprit, and somehow we have to find proof."

On that note, I left the room, leaving Barbara staring after me.

# Chapter 37

Late the next morning, drained from my run-in with Todd and Sergeant Plate, I took a calming glass of whiskey and ice out to my favourite tree stump and lit up a cigarette. Most times, this soothes me, but today I felt restless.

As I bent to stub out my cigarette, there came a stinging blow on the side of my head. It hurt like hell, and blood ran down the side of my face. The cigarette, along with the ashtray, fell to the ground. Had a branch from a tree fallen on my head? A massive crack on my shoulder knocked me off the log. The force of the blow pitched me onto the ground. Good heavens, what was happening?

Something whizzed by my head again, and I struggled to roll over onto my back. Emily Barraclough stood in front of me, the cane held over her head and an insane look in her eyes.

"Mrs B, what on earth are you doing, you batty old crone?" I yelled.

"Trying to kill you, Dimpy. Now be a good girl and keep still, I didn't realise this would be so hard. It's much easier to use poison."

"Are you mad? I'm not going to keep still while you hit me. You may as well put the cane down and tell me why you want me dead."

Terrified and in a great deal of pain, a thought went through my head. If I kept Mrs B talking, it might take her mind off the cane.

"I'm next in line for an apartment with a patio, and you're standing in my way. Put your head back down on the ground so I can hit it; there's a good girl."

"You want to kill me to have my apartment? Why didn't you ask me?"

"Would you have given it to me, Dimpy?"

"I'd have to think about it, can I think about it now?" Of course, I wouldn't give my apartment to her. However, lying on my back, dress up around my bum and in agony from a broken shoulder and cracked head, was not a good time for negotiations.

Fighting through tears brought on by the pain, I tried to reason with her again. "You won't get away with this. They'll find out it was you who killed me by the marks made by your cane."

"Oh, no, they won't. Everyone overheard your argument with Todd at the concert. He'll get the blame," she said, making another attempt to hit me and missing as I rolled out of the way. "I'll leave the cane in Judith's room and say I lost it." She snickered. "I don't need to use one anyway; it's only for show."

She lifted the cane above her head, ready to strike again. I rolled over and yelped from the intense pain in my shoulder. The cane crashed down, missing me by millimetres and hitting the log which sent bark flying everywhere.

A rustling sound came from inside the hollow log.

Mrs B stopped trying to hit me and looked at the log. "What was that noise?"

"Be careful, Emily, it might be a snake. They like hollow logs."

"Well, I'm not going to let a snake stop me, so take that." She slammed the cane down on the log.

Next minute the bandicoot streaked out, ran straight up Mrs B and latched her claws onto her face. She let out a scream, dropped the cane and began struggling to dislodge the bandicoot, which had become firmly fastened to her nose. "Get it off me, get it off me," she yelled.

I managed to get to my feet as the bandicoot let go and disappeared into the bush. Pain shot through my arm as I limped across to Mrs B. The effort became too much when I tripped over the cane and fell facedown across her legs. I heard a sharp crack and hoped it wasn't me.

"You stupid woman," Mrs B screamed, "you've broken my leg. Get off me you silly old cow."

Footsteps sounded as someone hurried towards us. The bushes parted, and Judith rushed into the clearing.

'What's all the yelling about? What on earth is going on here?" she said. "You're falling over people again, aren't you Dimpy ... and you're bleeding."

"Quick, Judith," I yelled while Mrs B tried to grab me by the throat. "Get Barbara, get the police and ring for an ambulance. Mrs B's gone crazy. She's trying to kill me." As an afterthought, I added, "oh yes, grab her cane and take it with you.'

Without another word, Judith nodded, picked up the cane and left the clearing calling out Barbara's name as she disappeared.

"Cane or no cane, I'm going to kill you, Dimpy, even if I have to kill myself first."

What a stupid thing to say, I thought as I hung onto her hands to keep them away from my throat.

What a sight we must have made, two old dears rolling around on the ground, one with a broken shoulder and the other with a fractured leg. What happened here would be the talk of the Manor for the next ten years ... if I could only keep her underneath me and not become another victim.

After what seemed like forever, my little haven came alive. First, with police officers, including Sergeant Plate and Constable McKellar, followed by Barbara, Judith, still holding the cane, Dianne, her husband Graeme, Carol and assorted residents and paramedics.

"Do you want me to sit on Mrs B while you get up Dimpy?" Carol called out in an anxious voice.

I felt a hysterical giggling fit coming on at the thought of fat Carol sitting on skinny Mrs B.

While trying to keep Mrs B from bucking me off, I managed to say, "No thanks, Carol. The police will deal with the old bitch."

Sergeant Plate clamped his hands onto Mrs B's shoulders and kept her still while Constable McKellar pulled me clear. Two paramedics took over, laid me on a stretcher and with gentle hands began to check my head and shoulder.

The sergeant battled to put handcuffs on Mrs B's wrists before lowering her onto another stretcher. It was a sorry sight to see as she sobbed and hiccupped. One of the paramedics gave her some tissues, which she snatched and used to dab at her sore nose where the bandicoot scratched her.

Sergeant Plate walked over to where I lay. "Fell over her, did you, Dimpy?" he tried to say in a solemn voice as he choked back a laugh.

With an indignant glare in his direction, I opened my mouth to explain.

He placed a hand on my good shoulder, and said, "Don't tell me now. I'm looking forward to an interview once the hospital has taken care of you."

"I'm glad you were here this morning and not at the police station."

"We don't usually work on Saturdays, and it was pure luck that Constable McKellar and I were here at the Manor. Mrs Wakefield had rung the police station late yesterday afternoon asking if I was available. I happened to be out of the office on another case, so Constable McKellar told her we would meet with her at the Manor this morning. We were discussing the information regarding your accusation that Mrs Barraclough was the murderer when a voice in the corridor began calling out Barbara Wakefield's name.

"Then this lady," he nodded in Judith's direction, "ran into the office waving a cane in the air and shouting Mrs B was trying to kill Dimpy and to call an ambulance. Barbara rang the paramedics while Constable McKellar and I followed this lady back here." He turned around and grinned. "It seems as though most of the residents have also arrived to find out what the commotion was about."

Barbara made her way towards us. "The ambulance will take you to hospital, Dimpy," she said. "According to the paramedics, you need x-rays for the wound on your head. They also think you have broken your shoulder blade."

A paramedic came over to us. "The other lady has a broken leg," he said. "It will need to be set back in position and plastered at the hospital."

"Well, I'm not going to the hospital with her," I said in a firm voice, "She tried to kill me, and I'm not giving her another chance in the ambulance."

Barbara sighed. "Would you go if I sat in the back of the ambulance, as well as a paramedic?"

"Okay, I guess ... as long as you sit between us so she can't reach me. At the hospital I want separate rooms, I'm not sharing with a homicidal maniac. What are you doing?" The last words were addressed to a man I could see bending over me with a needle in his hand.

"Giving you something to help with the pain," he said, stabbing me in the arm.

There was no time to tell the man needles caused me to pass out. Even watching someone else being vaccinated makes me weak at the knees. So, I fainted and didn't remember anything about the ride to the hospital.

Being x-rayed, then having my shoulder blade plastered and the cut on my head cleaned and patched took some time, but I was still awake when they wheeled me into a ward at the hospital.

That was the last I remembered until being woken up early the next morning to have my temperature checked, blood pressure read, and a new dressing put on my head. Later that morning, when I woke up again, Ronni, in her dressing gown, was bent over me, while Judith hovered behind her.

"We've brought your dressing gown, nightie, slippers and personal items. Are you sure you'll be okay now?" Ronni asked with an anxious look. "Is it true what Judith told me? That Mrs B tried to kill you?"

I nodded, still too tired and sore to speak.

"If there's anything else you need, let us know," Judith chimed in. "Ronni is your room-mate and will keep an eye on you."

I smiled at them, such good friends.

A huge yawn escaped. "Thank you both; I'm grateful for all the help you have given me." Another yawn, "After a good rest this morning, I'll tell you all about it."

"See you after lunch," Judith said as she left the room. Ronni picked up her towel and cosmetic bag and disappeared into the bathroom.

I went back to sleep.

## Chapter 38

After three days in the hospital, the doctor allowed me to go home. After lunch, Judith and Ronni, who had been released from the hospital a few days earlier, arrived in a taxi to take me back to the Manor.

As Judith told me the latest news about Todd, the nurse helped me dress in the clothes Ronni had brought in for me to change into.

"Yesterday Todd turned up at Dianne's house still smouldering about the Enduring Power of Attorney," Judith said. "Graeme spoke to him and said they would put the police onto him if he tried to bully me again. He stomped out, and nobody has seen or heard from him since."

Mm, my thoughts were that he would turn up again, most bad pennies do. But this time, Judith would not have to deal with him by herself. She had family and friends to help with Todd if he attempted to bully his mother again.

Ronni removed a parcel wrapped in pink cellophane with a purple bow from a large handbag. "This is for you," she said, giggling like a schoolgirl as she handed it to me.

"Open it straight away," Judith said with a grin.

Inside the parcel was a cotton shirt complete with collar, cuffs and a side pocket. Teal blue, my favourite colour. I held it up, one-handed to have a closer look at the writing on the pocket and began to laugh. "Thank you, both of you; this is just what the doctor ordered."

Embroidered on the pocket in black cursive handwriting were the words *'Bitchy Old Crone'*.

Ronni helped me remove my blouse and put on the polo shirt. It was a perfect fit. Then they opened their cardigans and paraded around the bed. Their shirts were the same as mine, but Ronni's was pink, and Judith's lime green.

Barbara appeared in the reception area when we arrived back at the Manor and came over to greet me. "Welcome home. I'd like to hug you, but it would most likely be a bad idea at the moment, so I'll save it until your arm has mended. By the way, love the shirts."

Some people came to the doors of their rooms as I walked down the corridor and called out 'pleased to see you home again' greetings. With a nod and a smile at everyone, I waited while Ronni opened the door to my apartment and ushered me inside.

But the exertion during the day had been tiring, and I needed a bit of me-time. Careful not to damage my shoulder blade, I hugged Ronni and Judith, then told them I wanted to lie down alone and rest for a while. They fussed me to the bed, and when I was comfortable, piled pillows behind my head. They made sure the plaster was in the correct position and draped a blanket over my legs. Then they tiptoed out the door, careful to close it softly behind them.

I waited a few minutes after the sound of their footsteps disappeared down the corridor, rose with some difficulty and walked into the kitchen. With exasperation from being one-handed, I reached for a glass and made a whiskey and soda, heavy on the whiskey.

After unlocking and opening the patio door, I shuffled back inside and picked up my drink. With the glass balanced in my left hand because the right shoulder blade was out of action, I limped down to my favourite spot in the clearing at the bottom of the garden. Once there, I slowly lowered myself down onto the log, being careful not to spill my drink.

After a large sip of the almost straight whiskey, I took a deep breath and looked around, relieved to see everything looked the same as usual. No bloodstains, no nasty woman with a lethal cane. You would never have known a maniac had attacked me here less than a week ago.

The dressing had been removed from my head, but the bruises on my back and legs were still blue and yellow, but as they were in places where no one could see them it didn't matter. They hurt a little bit when I walked, sat down or attempted to do anything physical. It would be another five weeks before my shoulder blade would be mended enough for the plaster to be removed.

I placed the glass on the ground beside me, then managed to reach into the log, pulled out the plastic bag containing a cigarette and lighter. Only using my good hand, I juggled a cigarette into my mouth and lit up. Holding the cigarette between the fingers of my right hand, I picked up the glass and began to sip.

As I relaxed, memories began to flood back.

# Chapter 39

Two days after the fight in the clearing, Sergeant Plate called into the hospital to discuss the results of the investigation.

"Emily Barraclough has been admitted to a private ward of the local psychiatric clinic under guard," he told me. "Her erratic behaviour has escalated, and she is at risk of harming herself."

"How was she able to kill two people and nearly murder three others, including me?"

"After her arrest and being questioned about the murders and accidents, Mrs B sang like the traditional canary. She boasted about what she had done."

"But how did she come to have those drugs that killed Barry and Don in the first place? Did she need to take them herself?"

"She had been a chemist's assistant for years, and when she retired, she took some of the drugs and poisonous substances with her. Unknown to anyone, she had a habit of visiting Barry in the early evening to have a bedtime glass of port with him. As she supplied the alcohol, he was happy to oblige. It was an easy matter for her to lace his port with digitalis."

"Mrs B once told me she didn't drink alcohol," I said, thinking of the time I saw her at the bottle shop.

"A lie in case you became suspicious."

"What did she do to Don?"

## A Manor of Murder

"As you know, Don did not like her, but he loved beer. She knocked on his door the night before he died with two cans of beer. They had been given to her as a present, she told Don, and because she didn't drink alcohol, she decided to give them to him."

Light dawned. These must have been the cans I saw her buy.

Sergeant Plate continued talking. "She asked herself in for a coffee. While he was in the kitchen, she opened a can and spiked it with the Warfarin tablets." A grim look and a sigh, then he said, "The worst part, Dimpy was that she sat and sipped her coffee while he drank the beer."

My voice was bitter as I replied. "What a terrible, cold-blooded thing to do." Then a thought occurred to me. "Her son is a pharmacist assistant in Launceston. Was he also involved?"

"He was stunned when his mother's antics came to light. We're convinced he had nothing what-so-ever to do with the deaths of Barry and Don and he was nowhere near the Manor when the accidents to Judith and Ronni occurred."

"Mrs B told me her son didn't have a dog. Was that true?"

"She never mentioned a dog when we spoke to her."

So, the incident with the dog in the park *had* been accidental and the owner an ignorant young man, not Mrs B's son.

"A thought niggled at me after Don died," I said. "Now, I remember what it was. Mrs B cradled the paper bag with both hands in front of her as she left the bottle shop. I should have noticed then that she walked out without her cane. When Mrs B attacked me in the clearing, she said the cane was only a prop."

"You're right; people tended to dismiss the idea of an old lady with a cane killing people. However, this one was special. It had belonged to her father, who needed a weighted cane to help him stand upright. Mrs B did not need to use a cane to walk. At least not all the time."

"Is that how she crept up on Judith and pushed her wheelchair down the hill?"

"Yes. She hid the cane under a bush, retrieved it after she pushed the wheelchair and hurried back in the other direction to the bus so she would have an alibi."

"Who would have thought Mrs B was such a crafty old bitch. What about the business with Judith and Todd?"

"Mrs B admitted everything. She was in the corridor when Todd stormed out. Judith's son is a nasty piece of work, already convicted of two counts of drunk driving and abusive behaviour to police officers."

"Judith was crying, so she returned to her room, put a bottle of sleeping pills in a pocket of her cardigan and came back to comfort her. She dissolved the pills into the milk in Judith's cup while a pot of tea brewed in the kitchenette. Mrs B shoved her out the glass door into the storm when she was nearly asleep but still able to function. Once done, she locked it, hoping Judith would get pneumonia and die."

"As for the poison in the coffee jar," he continued, "Mrs B overheard Ronni ask Molly to fill it while she went to the laundry. Molly put the empty jar on the bench near the kitchen to fill when she had a free moment".

"How did she manage to spike the coffee without anybody seeing her?"

"Easy. Lurking in the corridor as was her habit, she watched Mollie refill the jar with coffee. Then she went back to her room to get the strychnine. When Mrs B returned to the dining room, Molly had left to go shopping, and Ronni was still in the laundry. The coast was clear, so she slipped into the dining room, mixed strychnine with the coffee and placed the jar back where Molly had left it. From the entrance to the rec room, she saw Ronni enter the dining room, collect the jar and take it back to her room."

Sergeant Plate stopped talking for a moment and sighed. "Such a devious woman."

I nodded, and he continued, "We are not sure if she is batty or a schemer. But murdering people to get a patio apartment seems ridiculous. Either way, she is not going to be a problem for anyone else anymore."

While I was in the hospital, Barbara called in to give me the proof of my new novella which had arrived in the morning's mail. Being stuck in bed gave me a chance to read it through for errors. Once happy with both the cover and the story, I contacted the publisher to tell him I was pleased with the corrected manuscript. When he received the novellas from the printer, I would receive five free books. After keeping one for myself, signed copies would be given to Judith, Ronni and Barbara, and my family.

However, I still mourned the senseless deaths of Don and Barry. Thank goodness Ronni and Judith had survived.

I raised my glass and in a loud voice said, "To Barry and Don" and took a sip. Thinking about my new polo shirt, I held my glass up higher and declared in a more forceful voice, "Here's to the BITCHY OLD CRONIES."

There was a movement in the hollow log, and the bandicoot popped out and looked around. She spotted me and froze.

Smiling at her, I whispered, "Thank you, Mrs Bandicoot. I think you saved my life."

Good heavens. I rubbed my eyes. Yes, I'm positive I was not seeing things. Before she disappeared back into the log, the little bandicoot winked at me.

# About the Author

Wendy Laing is an Australian writer who lives in Deloraine, a small town on the island state of Tasmania. She is a member of the Society of Women Writers Tasmania and runs a local writing group.

*A Manor of Murder* is her second published novel, the first being *Memoirs of an Arresting Woman*.

# Also by Wendy Laing

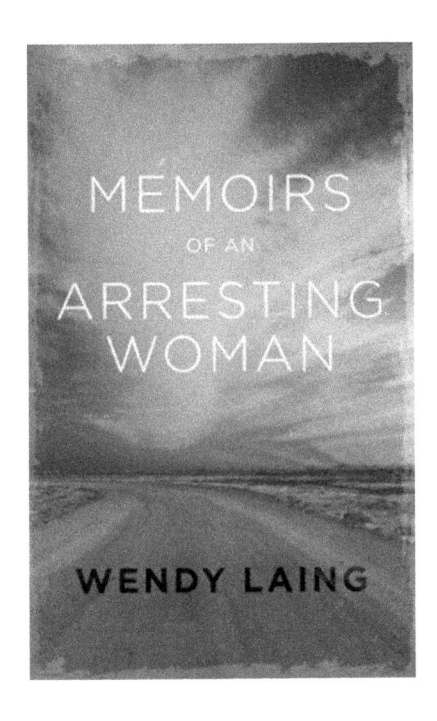

*Memoirs of an Arresting Woman*
Published by MoshPit
Publishing, March, 2019

In 1961, when Laurie McKenzie arrives in Darwin to take up a position as a constable, the Superintendent of Police informs her that because of an administrative error, she is the first and only female to be appointed as a police officer in the Northern Territory of Australia.

Laurie is posted to the outback mining town of Rabbit Creek where, as part of her job, she must deal with murders, a paedophile, a wife-beater and crocodile poachers, as she strives to earn the respect of the townspeople and her male colleagues.